Eleanor A Towle, Virginia Tennant, E. M Archer

Virginia Tennant

A novel. Part 2

Eleanor A Towle, Virginia Tennant, E. M Archer

Virginia Tennant
A novel. Part 2

ISBN/EAN: 9783337043773

Printed in Europe, USA, Canada, Australia, Japan

Cover: Foto ©Andreas Hilbeck / pixelio.de

More available books at **www.hansebooks.com**

VIRGINIA TENNANT

BY THE AUTHOR OF

"CHRISTINA NORTH," "A GOLDEN BAR,"
"BETWIXT MY LOVE AND ME,"

ETC. ETC.

'Where lies the land to which the ship would go?
Far, far ahead is all her seamen know.
And where the land she travels from? Away,
Far, far behind is all that they can say.'

IN TWO VOLUMES.

VOL. II.

LONDON:
HURST AND BLACKETT, LIMITED,
13, GREAT MARLBOROUGH STREET.
1888.

VIRGINIA TENNANT.

CHAPTER I.

IT was the middle of June. June roses were blooming outside in the garden ; and hung in clusters, red and white, about the windows ; a light wind blowing across the fields brought with it the fragrance of new-mown hay ; bees were busy amongst the clover ; and above the mist which veiled the low line of the horizon there stretched the blue arch of the unclouded heavens. Yet Virginia, who in other days had been wont to brave wind and storm rather than remain indoors, had not this afternoon been tempted out either by the roses or

the sunshine. She lay upon a low couch
in Lady Mainwaring's drawing-room, listlessly turning over the leaves of a novel.

It was five months since Colonel
Tennant died. They had been months of
slow and reluctant recovery from a malady
more wasting than any bodily disease. It
was what she had feared, and even yet she
hardly understood it. Death had been an
unknown enemy; never once, during her
twenty years of life, had she met him face
to face; and now the inexorable decree
of separation had gone forth, and it was in
vain that she stretched out longing hands
through the darkness.

She remembered but little of the first
hours after the blow had fallen. Lying
upon the bed to which they had carried
her, she knew that Mademoiselle Joseph
was sobbing behind a curtain, she felt the
water some one was sprinkling upon her
brow, she saw Norton Stansfield's dark
grave eyes regarding her from the door-

way. But she was a passive agent in other people's hands. She was in a dream, and prayed that she might not awake, for full consciousness would, as she dimly understood, bring remembrance in its train. Then she would know that he . . . 'Oh, God,' she cried, 'help me to forget.' She shuddered, and turned her face from the light. When they spoke, she did not answer. She did not want to hear what they might have to tell.

And yet she knew that all was over, that her hopes and fears were numbered with the dead—only a living sorrow cried aloud within her, and with each recurring pang proclaimed its immortality. With dull indifferent eyes she watched the flickering sunshine, as it lay in patches upon her bed-room floor; she touched the great bunch of roses which they brought her with careless fingers; the light had passed from the earth, the sweetness had left the flowers. The doctor came and looked at her, and talked of a nervous shock and feverish symptoms. She would have laughed at him if it had been worth while, but it was less troublesome to lie still and take the medicines which he sent her. She was not ill in body, and from the malady which was upon her she had no desire to be freed.

After a while they said that she was well enough to leave her room, and she made no objection, but dressed and came down to the drawing-room where Mrs. Stansfield was as usual adding up her accounts at her writing-table, and Emmeline bent her head discontentedly over a book. Virginia sat a little apart, she was still and uncomplaining, ready (far more ready than she had been) to defer to other people's wishes. She listened patiently to Emmeline, she acquiesced in her aunt's arrangements and looked with wondering pity at Mademoiselle Joseph's woe-begone countenance ; but her individuality was, as it were, obliterated

by a grief which had poisoned the very
well-springs of life. It was in vain for her
that nature clothed itself once more in all
the freshness of the spring, in vain that
the young leaves tossed their delicate ver-
dure against the summer skies. Wearily,
tearlessly, she let the days go by, but she
lay sobbing out her misery in the silence of
the night, or walked restlessly up and down
her room when others slept and the cold
moonlight lay across the floor.

Norton had been called away upon business, and Hartley (whose courtship could
not well be carried on under existing circumstances) was abroad; indeed, his mother
sometimes feared that his fluctuating
admiration might receive a shock if he
were to see Virginia pale and silent, a
shadow of her former self; and when Lady
Mainwaring expressed a wish to take the
girl away for a time Mrs. Stansfield caught
at her suggestion. The change of scene
would do her good, and by the time she

returned to Stansfield this season of inordinate sorrow would be passed. Virginia made no objection. All places were alike to her, but she thought that it was kind of Lady Mainwaring, and it would be good for Mademoiselle Joseph to be relieved from the painfully incessant watch she now kept over her. At Hinton, she, poor lady, would be more kindly treated than at Stansfield. So it had come to pass that she had been already several weeks under Lady Mainwaring's hospitable roof, and her kind hostess, seeing her still so languid and spiritless, would not hear of letting her return to her aunt's unsympathetic household. At any rate, here she could be indulged and cared for. The old lady had grown very fond of the girl, though she now seldom saw the smile which was so like her father's. There was a grace in her movements even in the slightest gestures, in the pose of her head, in the touch of her little hands which pleased Lady Mainwaring's fastidious taste. With all her freedom, Virginia had nothing in common with the girls whom Mademoiselle Joseph characterised as 'emancipated.' She had but little occasion for pride, holding those with whom she did not desire any closer contact at a distance by the more effectual shield of a careless indifference which she was at no pains to conceal. That Hartley had in some measure thrust the shield aside was due rather to the circumstances of the case than to his own strength or ability. Virginia had not yielded one inch of vantage-ground, and yet he had hurt her because he had presumed to set his foot upon it. She had not imagined that any-one would have dared to take from her what it was hers alone to give or to with-hold; for the moment he had almost succeeded in teaching her the lesson of distrust which, when once acquired, changes the aspect of the world around as a land-scape is transformed when seen through coloured glass; but that lesson was already forgotten, the blow which had fallen upon her had stunned her faculties of remembrance and thrown into insignificance all the other incidents of her life.

'Will you come out, Virginia?' asked Lady Mainwaring's voice at her elbow. 'Harry is anxious to drive you in the new dog-cart, and though I will not positively answer for your getting back safely, still, I know you are not afraid.'

Perhaps she spoke not without motive. In other days any chance of an adventure would have had its attractions for Colonel Tennant's daughter, more especially in combination with a fresh horse and a high dog-cart; but this afternoon she did not catch at the suggestion.

'I had not intended to go out,' she answered, turning her little head upon the pillows of the couch; 'but if you would like me to come with you——'

'My dear, do you imagine that Harry

would be likely to get *me* into the dog-cart?' cried the old lady. 'No, I am going to walk down later to the village. You may come with me if you wish it. But I believe that Norton Stansfield is coming this afternoon, and I shall wait to see him.'

'Mr. Stansfield?' cried Virginia, raising herself upon the sofa. 'Has he come back?'

A little colour came into her cheeks; a gleam of light, though but faint and fleeting, had pierced the shadows.

'Yes, and it is upon your business that he wishes to see me; so that, if you feel equal to it, it would be as well that you should see him too.'

She paused, and turned her sharp yet kindly glance upon the girl.

'But about my business?' asked Virginia, not noticing the last part of her sentence. 'What can he have to do with that? I did not know that I had any business.'

'Nothing has been arranged as yet,' answered the old lady, looking somewhat perturbed. 'You see, my dear child, you had no one to act for you, and so . . . '

'Yes, I know; I understand,' cried Virginia, shrinking down upon the sofa. The wound was so fresh, she could not bear even the lightest touch upon it. She had not as yet felt that she was alone in the world, she had not had time to think of that, but now it struck her with a sense of forlorn desolation. Lady Mainwaring was very kind. She had done her best. Emmeline even had shown her sympathy; Mademoiselle Joseph was devoted, but she could neither support nor advise her. No; as Lady Mainwaring had said, there was no one. When she was left alone she let her book fall to the ground and tears, which she rarely shed by day, gathered in her eyes. She had lain awake through many hours of the preceding night, and she was physically exhausted. It was the hottest hour of the afternoon; outside all was still, except for the long swish of a scythe in the meadow and the droning of insects amongst the flowers by the window. Virginia pillowed her head upon her hands; she thought of La Vallière, and fancied that she heard once more the murmur of the bees amongst the lime-trees; and then, with the tears yet wet upon her lashes, she fell asleep.

She was still sleeping an hour later when some one opened the drawing-room door, and with some hesitation advanced into the room. It was Norton Stansfield. For an instant he did not perceive her. The low couch was drawn up on one side of the window, and the curtains veiled it from the light. Yet, as he cast a quick glance round the room, his eyes rested upon it, and he came forward and stood looking down with a gravity so profound as to have an element of melancholy in it. She was sleeping as gently as a child; one

hand hung relaxed over the side of the
sofa; the soft waves of loosened hair over-
shadowed her brow; her cheeks were
faintly flushed, and yet sorrow had set his
ineffaccable seal upon her; even as he
looked, it seemed to him that she was
changed.

'Even she could not escape,' he muttered
to himself. 'Poor child!'

Perhaps some slight involuntary movement disturbed her, for she stirred uneasily with a faint murmur of 'Papa;'
then her blue eyes opened fully, and, recalled in an instant to the present, she
sat up with outstretched hands and a
smile sweet and frank as a child's upon
her mouth.

'So you have come back at last, Mr.
Stansfield. Oh, I am glad that you have
come back.'

He coloured a little as he sat down,
still keeping in his one of the little hands
she had held out to him.

'If I had known that,' he said, a little
unsteadily, 'I could hardly have stayed
away so long.'

'Yes, I am glad,' she repeated, 'and it
is so long since I have been glad about
anything;' and tears, but softer tears than
those she had shed before, rose to her
eyes. 'You have always understood
best . . . you see your step-mother and
sister—everyone has been very kind, but
after all I have only Mademoiselle Joseph,
and I cannot be so selfish as to make her
more unhappy than she is already. I feel
very lonely.'

She withdrew her hand from him and
turned her head aside that he might not
see her mouth was trembling.

'My poor child!' cried Norton, gently.
'It was no wonder.'

'Then you do not think me such a
coward after all?' She brushed away her
tears and smiled a little, but it was a
smile which cut him to the heart. 'I

began to think that all my courage had deserted me.'

'On the contrary, I am sure that you will be very courageous,' he answered. 'Lady Mainwaring has told me that you were willing to see me; and she wants you to have some air. She tells me that you stay too much indoors; will you make an effort and come out with me?'

'I will come;' but she rose a little wearily to her feet. 'I was to have walked with her, though she does not want me. Poor Lady Mainwaring!' cried Virginia, sighing.

'Why poor?'

'Oh, she has been so patient and forbearing,' said the girl, gratefully. 'So good to me and to my poor Mademoiselle Joseph. And I have made her such a bad return. I am grateful, but it is not gratitude that she wants. And one is very unreasonable; do you know, it is almost wearisome to feel that some one else is so

anxious to cheer you and make you happy.
It oppresses you.'

'Yes, I understand that perfectly,
though I cannot say,' smiling, 'that I have
been taught it by experience.'

'You mean that no one has cared to
make you happy?'

'No,' he answered, seriously, 'no one
has ever ventured upon so futile a
task.'

Virginia paused in the act of leaving
the room, and looked back at him with her
hand upon the door.

'I think that you are to be more pitied
than I am,' she said, gently, 'and yet a
little while ago I thought that no one in
this world could be so miserable; but it is
worse for you to have nothing to remember, nothing to look back upon.'

'Then you pity me?'

'No!' cried Virginia, shaking her head in
her old manner. 'No, I do not pity you.
One pities only that which is weaker than

oneself. I do not pity, but I am sorry for you.'

She went to fetch her hat, and Lady Mainwaring entered at the same moment by the garden door.

'And how do you find Virginia?' she asked, regarding him with a scrutiny as searching but less kindly than that which she had cast upon the girl. 'She is greatly altered.

'Yes, she is altered,' answered Mr. Stansfield, shortly.

'And have you told her?'

'Why should I tell her?' he answered, gloomily; 'bad news, even when it is true, travels quickly enough; and I am especially anxious that Mrs. Stansfield at least should hear nothing of it at present.'

'Certainly you are right there, but then it is another matter as to Virginia.'

'You think that the knowledge of her loss of fortune might do her good?' he questioned. 'Perhaps you are right, but I must be guided by circumstances; there are other questions involved, and as one of her trustees . . .'

'You appear to regard yourself as her sole guardian,' interrupted the old lady, rather sharply.

'If I should do so no one, as far as I can see, is likely to interfere with my office,' answered Mr. Stansfield, calmly. 'I confess I was not prepared for the absolute indifference with which even men of business like Messrs. Everard regarded her losses. After all, Everard was a friend of her father's.'

'And has proved his worst enemy?'

'He has proved his own enemy as well. He is practically ruined.'

'And consequently has no thoughts to spare for Virginia. What is to become of her?' cried Lady Mainwaring, sitting down in a good deal of perturbation, and turning a diamond hoop about upon one of her fingers.

Mr. Stansfield was silent. It might have been from perplexity or from indifference; at any rate, he had no answer ready.

'It is a terrible position,' continued the old lady, naturally taking an exaggerated view of the matter under the influence of Norton's calmness. 'She is too young and pretty to be thrown upon the world; Mrs. Stansfield, you may be sure, will no longer be anxious to give her a home. And Virginia is too proud to be dependent upon anyone. I doubt if she would even remain with me.'

Mr. Stansfield had no doubts whatever upon that point; he was certain of it, and he said so.

'Then where is she to go?' cried Lady Mainwaring. 'I must say you take it very quietly. If, as you say, you are one of her trustees, it is your duty to speak, it is your duty to see what can be done.'

'I will endeavour to fulfil my duty,' he answered, with a slight smile.

'You seem to be very confident,' cried the old lady, irritably. 'You are not afraid of the responsibility you are undertaking. You think highly of yourself.'

'Since no one else will do so, it has become almost a necessity,' he answered, with some bitterness.

'No, Norton, do not say that;' and she looked up at him kindly. 'I am a rough-spoken old woman, but I never distrusted you. I always said that you were true. Very moody and unreasonable and sulky, you know, but still true. I am sorry for you, Norton, you are like a fruit which might have been ripened by sunshine, but which has grown hard and bitter because . . .'

'Because?' he questioned, as she paused for a word. 'Surely the cause is not so far to seek. Have I not been always an obstacle, an involuntary one, I grant

c 2

you, but still an obstacle in other people's
way. Who at Stansfield, until this
poor child came amongst us, has ever
cared for my interests, or looked upon me
as anything but an enemy?'

'Yes, I know that was their view, and
I suppose you thought it necessary to
justify it,' said Lady Mainwaring, sharply.

'Not exactly;' and again he smiled a
little, the old lady's brusqueness rather
amused him. 'I had very little to do
with the matter. But it was a surprise,
a great surprise to be regarded as a
friend.'

'Yes, Virginia is so confident, she has no
fears, no reserve. She is ready to believe
in everyone, and yet she is not wanting in
discernment. It is not easy to conceal
anything from her. Perhaps it might
be best, after all, to lay her own case
before her. I hate the task, yet I would
explain matters to her if you thought it
best.'

'On no account,' he cried, quickly. 'If she must be told, I will tell her myself.'

'As you please,' she answered, a little offended.

'And it will not be until I have seen Mr. Everard again and made quite sure of my facts.'

He stopped short as Virginia came into the room and stood still upon the threshold looking a little enquiringly from one to the other.

'Were you talking about me?' she asked, gently.

'We were,' answered Mr. Stansfield, 'but we are not yet prepared to take you into our counsels. Let us,' stretching out his hand to her—'Let us go into the garden.'

'Yes, I am right, Norton is true, one can trust him, and yet I am glad that he clearly regards Virginia as a child,' said Lady Mainwaring to herself. 'He will care for her interests as an elder brother, and that

is best.   It would be dangerous to have a
man of his uncertain temper and moody
temperament for a lover.   It is best as it
is.'

CHAPTER II.

'VIRGINIA must come home,' said Mrs. Stansfield, gathering up her letters with an air of vexation as she rose from the breakfast-table.'

Emmeline was still seated at it listlessly playing with her teaspoon. She did not look up as she murmured,

'I am sure I wish that she would.' There was discontent undefined yet deep-seated in her tone, her attitude, her aspect. The months that had passed had not exercised a good influence upon her character. For awhile she had been roused from her apathetic self-occupation, she had been really sorry, genuinely sorry for a misfortune not her own, but when the emergency

had passed away the recoil from these un-
pleasing and unnecessary emotions had
been all the greater, and left alone with
Mrs. Stansfield she had fallen back into
weaker health and more complaining
spirits. She had no energy to occupy herself with books at home; no inclination to
seek distractions abroad. Norton's return
was a grievance, and Virginia's continued
absence an annoyance. Altogether Miss
Stansfield felt herself to have been injured
by Colonel Tennant's death. She had
been very fairly well and happy before,
now everyone and everything united to
make her uncomfortable. The weather too
was insufferably hot, and served to aggra-
vate her feelings.

'Yes, I wish that Virginia would come
back; yet I am sure I do not know why I
should wish it,' she repeated. 'I think she
has grown very selfish. She has not been
to ask after me for weeks. I daresay she
finds it pleasanter to have nothing to do

but to be indulged by Lady Mainwaring. After all, other people have had their troubles as well as Virginia. I am sure I don't know, now I come to think of it, why we made such a fuss about hers.'

'I wish that you would try to attach your cousin instead of grumbling at her,' answered Mrs. Stansfield. She looked unusually perturbed, and sat down again with an absence of her usual decision. As a rule, when Mrs. Stansfield was about to leave the room, nothing would have delayed her in any way. She carried a resolution worthy of greater matters into the smallest details of life. 'I wish you could see something beyond your own immediate interests. I think that it is I who am very badly used. Norton will hardly open his lips to me about the girl's future, and though for some inscrutable reason my brother made him his trustee it is surely natural that he should consult me about my own niece's affairs. He has been

to see Mr. Everard again this week. I do
not understand it.'

'Why should we understand it, mamma?
I am sure business is always a great bore.
It is the most disagreeable thing in the
world. Why should we wish to have anything to do with it ?'

'How can one avoid it ?' asked her
mother, impatiently. 'Here are the most
unsatisfactory accounts of Hartley. He is
wanting money again, and how am I to
send it to him? It is absolutely necessary
that he should come home.'

'And marry Virginia ?' asked Emmeline,
raising her eyebrows. 'Dear me, mamma,
are you harping again upon that old
string? I thought that it was broken
long ago.'

'I believe Virginia has been left extremely well off, though Norton is so
reserved upon the subject,' continued Mrs.
Stansfield, pursuing her own train of
thought. 'It is a most unfortunate

position for a girl unless she has some one to take care of her, she is certain to fall a prey to some needy fortune-hunter.'

'At any rate she will not fall a prey to Hartley, and evils are comparative,' answered Emmeline, drily.

But her mother was too much absorbed in her own thoughts to heed her.

'We must first induce Virginia to return here,' she said. 'I can truly say that I shall feel hurt if she remains away any longer. It is very wrong of Lady Mainwaring to encourage her. You must drive over with me to Hinton, Emmeline, and we will persuade her to come back.'

'We should not be likely to succeed, and it is too hot to exert oneself. It would make me positively ill to drive out in this sun. No, my dear mamma, you must think of some other plan. You had better send Norton.'

'Norton!—why, what influence could he have?'

'Virginia likes him,' answered Miss
Stansfield. 'It is very unaccountable,
but she certainly likes him, and, what is
even more wonderful, I believe he has
been very kind to her.'

Mrs. Stansfield made no answer, but she
looked as if the suggestion were an unpleasant one. Now that she thought of it,
it seemed to her that since his return
Norton had been somewhat changed. Not
less grave, but gentler, happier, and less
moody. Could Virginia by any possibility
have caused this change? yet this supposi-
tion was hardly compatible with her dis-
inclination to return to Stansfield.

Mrs. Stansfield went to the French window, and, pushing it open, stepped out
on to the terrace. Two figures were just
parting from one another at the corner of
the shrubbery, and Mr. Stansfield came
towards her, whilst Marshall walked away
in an opposite direction.

Mr. Stansfield looked undisturbed as

usual, yet his first words betrayed some
discomposure.

'I have had to come to an understanding
with Marshall,' he said. 'I could tolerate
his unreasonable animosity to me, but
when he carries his prejudices into matters
which concern the good of the property it
becomes unbearable. I have told him that
I cannot retain him in his present position,
and he has walked away venting some
mysterious threats which he evidently
expected to have a great effect upon me;'
and he laughed but with some annoyance.
'The man is a monomaniac.'

'He is perfectly invaluable to me,' answered Mrs. Stansfield, reddening with
anger. '*I* shall at any rate retain him as
my man of business. You can hardly
object to that.'

'Certainly not, only if he should prove
untrustworthy please remember that I
warned you. He is more fool than villain,
but for all practical purposes I should

prefer a villain. Did not I hear that his mother was insane?'

'Really I cannot say,' answered Mrs. Stansfield, vainly endeavouring to hide her discomfiture. Marshall's dismissal at this moment was particularly inconvenient, yet she saw that it would be in vain to plead his cause. 'I do not think it necessary to study the antecedents of everyone that I have about me. I consider him to be a clear-headed and useful servant, and as such I decline to part with him.'

'As you please,' he answered, indifferently. 'He will not now be in a position to do any injury to the estate. As to the rest, if you choose to retain him as your servant, you must take the consequences and remember that I have warned you. To turn to another subject, what is the meaning of this letter from Jack?' and he held out a scrawled sheet of paper torn from an exercise-book.

'DEAR NORTON,

'It is a beastly shame that they won't let me come home. The school will never forget it if I am kept here through the holidays. Some injuries are bound to be revenged; and I do not think that they will find that " revenge is sweet." If you will get me sent for to Stansfield I will fight on your side for the rest of my life. Ask Virginia if I should not be a comfort to her. Write by return.

'Your affectionate brother,

'JACK.'

'It means that I intended to leave Jack at school during these holidays,' answered Mrs. Stansfield, grimly, returning the letter. 'He gets more idle every term, and I am not equal to the hourly anxiety he causes me when he is at home. Life when Jack is in the house becomes a series of unpleasant surprises.'

'Still, is it not a choice of evils? It strikes me that if you leave him at school you will have a heavy bill for damages.'

'It is impossible to know what to do with such a boy,' cried the aggrieved mother; 'last time he was here he rode postilion through Hyde on one of the carriage horses. I was seated in the brougham quietly looking over some papers and I could not conceive why half the population seemed to be running out to look at us. I might just as well have been driving through the town with a circus troupe; and the coachman was actually laughing! I gave him notice to leave that evening, and I have never had such a good servant in the stables since. It is too annoying.'

'He will hardly repeat that form of annoyance,' observed Norton. 'I think if I were you I should revoke your sentence of banishment. Emmeline tells me that you want Virginia to come back, and do you know I believe that Jack is right, he will be a consolation to her.   She likes the boy.'

'She is such a child herself,' said Mrs. Stansfield; but yet she was gratified. Even if one has reared an ugly duckling, it is a natural maternal instinct to be pleased if other people admire it.   Jack was insufferable, still she was glad that some one could find it possible to like him.   It was very odd, he certainly had shown a desire to be in Virginia's company; she had actually sat in his workshop amongst his glue-pots and horribly-smelling chemicals, and she had found them on the rug before the fire telling each other stories in the twilight.   Mrs. Stansfield could not doubt that if Virginia found him away when she returned she would be disappointed.   So, after all, that evening Norton sent his half-brother, together with a postal order, permission to return as usual for the midsummer vacation.

'Short but sweet,' cried Master Jack, surveying the amount of the order with a good deal of satisfaction. 'Norton knows what is right. He does not do things by halves. I call these,' tucking the money into his trowsers pocket—'I call these supplies voted for secret service. The authorized revenue being so wretchedly inadequate, if it were not for them the exchequer would be empty.'

CHAPTER III.

'WHEN will you come home?' asked Norton
Stansfield.

'If you want Virginia to come back you
must send Norton to fetch her;' so Emmeline had said, but her mother had not
taken her advice; it was not part of her
plan to make her step-son her ambassador;
nevertheless, he had come upon his own
business, and without any reference to
other people he profferred his request.

Virginia raised her eyes to him and shook
her head.

'Home?' she said, a little unsteadily.

It was towards evening. The shadows
of the 'straight line of cypresses which
hedged the lawn to westward lay long upon

the turf; above them the clear transparent reach of sky was crossed by sunset lights. Virginia sat on a low stone bench, her hands were loosely clasped together over the folds of her black dress, one small foot crept out beneath it and was idly stirring the pebbles.

Mr. Stansfield seated himself beside her, leaning one arm upon the bench.

'Shall I put the question in another form? When are you coming back to Stansfield?'

'You seem to be quite certain,' said Virginia, looking up and laughing a little. 'You appear to have no doubt that I shall come back some time.'

'I have no doubt. It would be unlike you to stay away.'

'Unlike me. Mr. Stansfield, do you think that you know what would be unlike me? Do you think that you know what I am like?'

He sat still gravely considering her, with

eyes that had a curious latent expression not easy to define.

'Have you ever seen a dawn in a summer sky?' he answered, a little irrelevantly.

'Often, yes, but what has that to do with me?'

He put that question aside.

'I think that you will come back to Stansfield,' he said, 'you are wanted there.'

'I wish that I could believe it, it is pleasant to be wanted, and yet—I should not like to be a necessary of life. It is too great a responsibility. It is not one that I am likely to incur now;' and she sighed a little. 'Mr. Stansfield, why do you say that I am wanted at your house?'

'Perhaps because it is my house,' he said, with a gleam in his dark eyes. 'Is it quite,' he hesitated an instant for a word, 'is it quite courageous of you to stay away?'

She flushed a little and was silent.

'I told you that I had not much courage left,' she said at last, 'and just now it is easier to think of the present than of the future. When I look on, I see a blank wall before me, and—I do not feel strong enough to climb over it. I could not always remain at Stansfield: I will go back now if you wish it, but I could not always remain there.'

'What do *you* wish?' he questioned, gently.

'I hardly know. I was very wicked a little while ago. I wished that it were all over; that I need not live on here alone; and when I was ill and weak it seemed easy to slip out of life; but it was a great mistake, I am not fit to die.'

'God forbid,' he cried, involuntarily. 'God forbid.'

He glanced for an instant at her slight young figure, at the fair serious brows under the shade of the wide hat which still

had the pure and untroubled aspect of a
child's and meeting the surprise in her
eyes he turned hastily away.   Between the
tops of the tall cypresses the sky showed
its pale background of harebell blue;
the evening breeze stirred, and swept an
acacia branch aside, but was too gentle
to pierce their denser foliage.   Virginia
stretched out her hand, and, drawing down
one of the near branches, absently plucked
a spray, and was fastening it in her dress,
when Norton laid his hand upon it.

'What do you mean?' he asked, angrily.
'One moment you talk of dying, and the
next instant you gather cypress.'

'I shall if I please,' cried Virginia, frightened into defiance.

'Indeed you shall not,' easily detaching
her small fingers from the ominous token
and flinging it to a distance.   'You shall
have nothing to do with it.   Well, are
you angry with me?   What are you thinking of?'

For she had coloured either in confusion or anger, as she drew her hands away, and she would not raise her eyes.

'I was thinking that your step-mother was right,' she said at last, 'when she declared that you always wanted to be master.'

'Sometimes—not always.'

'And, as you are at present in Lady Mainwaring's garden, I do not think that it is quite proper,' continued the girl, standing up to shake some scattered leaves from her dress.

'Let us leave that question then for the present,' he said, laughing a little. 'And let me have an answer to the more important one; are you angry with me?'

'A little,' answered Virginia, smiling. 'But I am afraid that my anger is not a very formidable thing.'

'It is to me, I assure you. It is only for your own good that I would venture to incur it.'

'My own good,' she echoed, 'and who is to be the judge of that? Do you know, Mr. Stansfield, I used to think that I knew what was good for me.'

'And you made mistakes, and would do so again.'

'At any rate I am less likely to make them than anyone else. How should you, for instance, be able to judge for me?'

'Would you not trust me?' he asked. He spoke more gravely than the occasion seemed to demand, and she made him no answer for one or two moments.

'How trust you? Yes, certainly I would trust you; but I suppose even you will allow that it is conceivable that under certain circumstances I might know best.'

'Why do you say that " even I " might concede so much as that?'

'Because I think that you have but a poor opinion of me,' answered Virginia, lightly pulling the petals from a daisy.

'It is true I had not much experience.'

'Do not regret that,' he cried, quickly, 'experience is a hard schoolmaster. My rule would be lighter than his.'

'A beneficent despotism?' and she looked up with a frank laugh. 'But I am not yet prepared to swear allegiance.'

Norton made no answer, and in silence they passed together down a shrubbery walk. Thick branches overhead shut out the level rays of the sunset; the air was faint with the heavy scent of the Portugal laurels. Virginia walked along slowly, with her eyes upon the ground; a shadow had fallen upon her spirits, and her thoughts once more were sadly twining themselves about the past.

'Is it not wonderful,' she said, presently, in a low voice, 'that one changes so soon. It is true, at first, I wished that I too were dead. It seemed impossible to go on living; and now it is not that one *forgets;* I could not forget, but still one is glad of the summer, and of so many things. I can,' remorsefully, whilst tears gathered in her eyes, ' I can still be happy.'

Her words stirred some long-forgotten memories. He too remembered a time when he believed that sorrow and joy were alike eternal. There are some illusions for which one would pay a heavy price.

' Does nothing last?' asked the girl, a little drearily. ' Must everything sooner or later change and alter? May we not hope to keep anything?'

' Nothing,' he made answer within himself, and looking down at her he sighed, but would not speak his thought aloud. ' Only one thing is eternal,' he said.

' Yes, love is eternal,' she answered. ' I do not forget it; death cannot take that from one, and yet . . .'

' I know,' he said, kindly. ' It is as you said, you are very lonely. But it will be better for you to return to Stansfield.

Here you are only a guest, you have,' smiling, 'your own way in everything. There you will have some daily duties and very likely trials.'

'But that does not encourage me to come back,' cried Virginia, brushing away her tears.

'Not even if I am there to smooth your path?'

'I am sure that you will do that,' she answered, gratefully. 'Indeed, if it were in your power, I believe these trials which you appear to value so highly would be altogether swept away. But I do not imagine that they would vex me now. Even Hartley would not trouble me.'

'He shall not,' he said, rather hastily; then, in another tone, 'He happens to be away at present.'

'And I shall not be long at Stansfield. No, you need not contradict me; upon that point my mind is made up. Mrs. Stansfield only tolerates me, Emmeline does not need me, and Hartley cannot live at home if I am there. Three very good reasons,' checking them off on her fingers, 'three very good reasons why I should go away.'

' Where do you propose to go ?' he asked, looking away from her.

' The world is wide ;' and she sighed a little. 'I am glad, yes,' emphatically, ' very glad that I am not penniless. It is absurd to despise money; I always said that I was very glad to be rich, and now I am more glad than ever. At any rate, I need not be a burden upon anyone.'

' You would dislike that.'

'I should detest it,' she answered, quickly. 'One must love some one very much if one can bear to be dependent upon them ; and I could not earn my daily bread; I cannot boast of one single useful accomplishment. Oh stay, I can make excellent pastry, for our old French cook taught me, but unluckily one cannot live upon sweetmeats.'

'Not even upon meringues?' asked Mr. Stansfield, rather quickly.

'How often your mind reverts to that episode in the library,' cried Virginia, laughing. 'One would imagine that it must be the only good action of your life, since it stands out so clearly. But to come back to the present, or rather to the future, I think that I will go back to La Vallière. It will make Mademoiselle Joseph very happy to see her poor friends in the village and kneel in the little church once more; and I love the old house and the wilderness of garden and the avenue of limes.'

'Yet you would be very solitary there.'

'Where should I not be solitary?' and her voice trembled. 'Why do you remind me of that?'

'Because I would not have you in such haste to leave us. Besides, I have certain rights; do you know that I am your trustee, and practically your sole guardian?'

'I thought that Mr. Everard ...' she

began, and stopped herself, colouring in a good deal of confusion.

' Mr. Everard has in a great measure devolved his responsibilities upon me. Does this,' bending to look at her under the shadow of her hat—' does this,' smiling, ' displease you ?'

' I am not sure,' answered Virginia, still with her eyes upon the ground, ' I think that I prefer to take care of myself. But if you have the charge of my affairs,' rallying her spirits, ' I should like you to get me some money. Mademoiselle Joseph has been unaccountably niggardly of late, and my purse is nearly empty.'

' I will write to Mr. Everard and your needs shall be supplied,' he answered, quietly, ' and in return you shall prepare Lady Mainwaring for your departure.'

' An act of bare justice demands no return,' observed Virginia, decidedly, ' but perhaps you are right. I will come back.'

They had reached the border of the

shrubbery. Before them the lawn sloped down to a running stream which separated it from the meadows of the home farm. The grass had not yet been cut, and the gold and red of the high butter-cups and sorel burned in the sunset; over the distant woods the shadows of the departing day were already softly falling.

'Virginia, Virginia,' some one was calling in the distance. She wished Mr. Stansfield good-night and went back to the house. As he turned to follow her he met Mademoiselle Joseph advancing from the shelter of the shrubberies. He raised his hat and wished her good-morning somewhat coldly, not overpleased to perceive that she must have been furtively watching them, though not within earshot. But she put herself in his way with a deprecating gesture.

'Have you told her? My poor child, does she know?' she inquired tremulously.

'I have told her nothing except that she must come back to Stansfield,' he answered, shortly. 'I am very sorry, as you know, that Mr. Everard should have thought it necessary to trouble you. I trust, however, you have not made any communication to Mrs. Stansfield.'

'I do not think it is needful to remind me of Colonel Tennant's wishes;' and the old lady drew herself up. 'I have made no communications to anyone. But I am placed in a terrible position, Mr. Stansfield. She, remaining in complete ignorance, has no fears, but how can I help fearing for her. I have not even a home, however humble, of my own to which to take her. I understand that La Vallière remains to her, and the old servants are pensioned; but she cannot live there upon nothing, and Lady Mainwaring, who alone knows all, has no advice to offer. Even this courageous lady cannot advise me; and here is Virginia who says to me: "At least we are rich; we need not be dependent upon anyone. We must make a

home of our own, dear mademoiselle. Shall
we return to La Vallière ?" How am I to
answer her ?'

But Mr. Stansfield remained unmoved
and unsympathetic ; he even smiled a little
at the old lady's dismay.

'We must have patience, Mademoiselle
Joseph. You must tell her that her
business affairs are not yet settled. That
is so true a subterfuge that it need not
oppress your conscience. Possibly matters
are not so bad after all.'

But poor Mademoiselle Joseph shook her
head. Her health was not so good as it
had been ; she was conscious of being but
a faint-hearted and inefficient guardian, and
yet if she failed who would remain to Virginia ? She distrusted Mrs. Stansfield, she
despised Hartley, she did not understand
Mr. Norton Stansfield. She was a stranger
in a strange land, and slowly drawing out
her handkerchief she wiped away some
tears.

'Do not take it so much to heart,' observed Mr. Stansfield, kindly, though he still to all appearance had no share in her trouble. 'It is never worth while to grieve over misfortunes which are in the future. I can assure you that there will be no difficulty for the present in supplying you and Miss Tennant with anything that you need. I will give Mr. Everard instructions at once. I am very sorry to learn that you have suffered even a temporary inconvenience.'

'But he informed me that it was useless to apply to him,' cried the poor governess, disconsolately, 'and Virginia, you see, has never been used to be denied. I could not tell her the state of the case. I could only give her the little ready money which I had, not knowing where I could obtain any further supplies.'

'In fact, not knowing that you would ever be repaid?'

'It is not a question of repayment be-

E 2

tween me and Virginia,' cried Mademoiselle
Joseph, reddening. 'What little I have . . .'

'Forgive me,' answered Mr. Stansfield,
feeling somewhat rebuked. 'I did not
intend to imply that her obligations to you
could be measured. But will you try to
believe that you are not her only friend.
You know that Colonel Tennant at least
saw fit to trust me. Will you do so also?
There must be a period of uncertainty, but
when I have any solution of the difficulty
to offer you shall be told of it. Will that
satisfy you?'

Mademoiselle Joseph hesitated for a moment. Her furtive anxious gaze was lifted
to his countenance, whilst he stood still
and serious submitting himself to her
scrutiny. She saw dark eyes not frank,
indeed, but at once searching, and inscrutable; a mouth half hidden under a brown
beard, and an air of indifferent reserve
which sat naturally upon his handsome
features, and her heart failed her; but

when, seeing her manifest discomfiture, he smiled, and held out his hand, her spirits revived.

' Believe me, you are not to be left alone in your charge, mademoiselle.'

And she murmured more cheerfully : 'Ah! I believe you are good. You would not deceive us. I leave it in your hands.'

But when she had left him, and Norton was walking alone along the field footpaths towards Stansfield, there was a cloud upon his brow, a perplexity far greater than any which had presented itself to Mademoiselle Joseph's narrower vision lay upon his mind. His thoughts weaved themselves round and round about it, and as it were caught him in their snares. He could save Virginia from the ruin which threatened her only upon one condition, and to ask her to fulfil it would be like presenting terms of peace to a prisoner of war at the point of a bayonet. In one sense she was in his power, for she had no other refuge, and

after all he would require but one sacrifice,
the sacrifice of her freedom in return for a
captivity as sweet as he could make it, a shelter safe from all enemies without, of which
he alone would hold the key.   And yet he
had sufficient experience to be aware that
even a willing hostage is apt to chafe against
confinement ; and what is marriage but
bondage to a woman unless she loves, and
Virginia was so young she had not had
time as yet to weary of her liberty.   He
knew it so well, he would never have taken
the step which he had contemplated unless
circumstances had combined to make it
almost inevitable ; and yet would he have
foregone them ? No, not for a king's
ransom.

He glanced for an instant at the sky
now deepening under the evening lights
above the red irregular roofs and gables of
Stansfield ; under these quiet English skies,
beneath the shelter of the old house, Virginia should be cherished and guarded, and,

as far as it lay in his power to make it so, her fate should be a happy one. He was not a man to doubt his own power; nevertheless, he knew that a caged bird, however carefully tended, may flutter and beat itself to death against the bars.

' One must love some one very much if one can bear to be dependent upon them.' He recalled her words, and said to himself that for the present at least she should not know. Some day, some day he might tell her.

It was past the ordinary dinner-hour, and he went straight to the library and ordered dinner in his own rooms. He had no wish to join the family circle that evening, so he sat in his solitude far into the night looking into a girl's wet blue eyes as if he would find an answer to the question which he was asking there.

CHAPTER IV.

It was raining in torrents. The trees bowed beneath the gusts of wind, and even the strong young leaves were torn and whirled along the approach, whilst the old branches snapped and groaned under the storm. Every now and then a flash of lightning lit up the woods and pastures with a vivid unnatural glare, and the thunder crackled above the chimneys of the house. All the blinds were drawn in the drawing-room, and Emmeline Stansfield lay upon a sofa in the darkest corner with a shawl wrapped round her head.

'My nerves are utterly disorganized,' she murmured.

'Why, Emmeline, what is the matter? there is nothing to be afraid of,' cried Jack, marching into the room in muddy boots and a dripping jacket. 'Don't be afraid, I'll take the fire-irons,' clattering them loudly, 'out of the fender, and then if the lightning does come down the chimney it won't do much damage. Don't be afraid.'

'Is it that forked kind?' asked his sister, shivering.

'Forked! why, the sky is all split up with it. It struck a man in the field just now and half of him was a cinder in a minute. But he is not dead yet, so you needn't be afraid. Oh, oh!' suddenly jumping off the floor like a Jack-in-a-box. —'Oh, what a clap!'

'Do shut the shutters,' implored Miss Stansfield, pressing her fingers to her ears. 'The thunder seems to have got inside the house. It must be right above us.'

'But I am so awfully frightened,' answered the boy, advancing cautiously on tiptoe towards the windows. 'No, Emmeline, I really cannot stand here to shut the shutters, it is asking too much. Why,' peeping behind the curtains, 'the fire is running all along the ground. It is better than the fireworks at Hyde on the 5th of November. What a bonfire this house would make, with all its old rafters; but I don't think it is at all likely to be struck, so don't be afraid, only I must say I wish Norton had listened to me and had put on a lightning conductor.'

'Yes, that is just like Norton, he never will listen to anybody. Dear me, Jack, do you hear the chimneys shaking?'

'Never mind. If the great stack falls, it will come right into the middle of the floor, it is not at all likely to hit you in that corner,' cried Jack, reassuringly. 'But I should draw up my feet a little further, if I were you, so as to make quite sure.'

'No, I really cannot stay here. I am getting quite ill;' and she sat up, looking pale and nervous. 'Ring the bell, Jack, ring twice for Martin.'

'Now, see how ignorant you are!' cried Jack. 'It is very dangerous to touch bells in a thunderstorm. It has something to do with the wires and electricity. Besides, it would not be of the slightest use, the maids are all in hysterics in the cellar. If you would like to join them I will take you; only we must cross the hall, and the skylight is sure to be blown in; still, it is not likely to fall on our heads, and I will go first, so you need not be afraid.'

'You wicked boy, you are doing your best to frighten me. It is very hard that no one pays me the least attention. Why, listen, surely that is the hall bell. Who can be arriving in this weather?'

'Only witches on broomsticks, I should imagine,' observed Master Jack, who, however, in his turn, looked somewhat startled. 'But why they should ring the front door bell is more than I can tell you.'

Yet, as they listened through the noise of the storm, the sounds of an arrival in the hall were plainly discernible, and in a few minutes Virginia entered, looking pale indeed in her deep mourning, but otherwise undisturbed.

'Why, how did you come?' exclaimed her cousin, forgetting her fears in her amazement.

'In the carriage,' answered the girl, composedly. 'It was not so bad when we started. Afterwards the horses were rather frightened, and thunder always affects Mademoiselle Joseph's nerves. She hopes that you will excuse her, she has gone to her own room. Oh, Jack,' turning to the boy, 'I am very glad that you are at home.'

'You are singular in your feelings, but they do you honour,' muttered Jack, who felt shy of her pale face and her mourning.

'And how are you, Emmeline?' continued Virginia. 'Does your head still ache. I am very sorry.'

'I am quite ill from the storm,' answered Miss Stansfield, sinking back upon her pillows. 'The atmospheric disturbance is enough to upset me, even putting the danger out of question.'

'Danger?' repeated Virginia, looking rather puzzled.

'Yes, when a man has been struck by lightning at our doors; when chimneys shake and the skylight is blown in, it is certainly no exaggeration to talk of danger.'

'The skylight blown in and a chimney struck! Oh, Jack,' looking round at her cousin, who had assumed an air of preternatural gravity. 'I give you up. You are a very bad boy.'

'But I kept telling her not to be afraid;

what could I do more?' asked the boy.
' Is it not true, Emmeline ; did I not say
to you over and over again, don't be afraid.
The skylight will not fall upon you, the
chimneys will be sure to miss the sofa ;
don't be afraid. But you would not
believe me.'

' Oh, look ! there is another flash,' cried
Miss Stansfield, not heeding him. ' It is
not over.'

' It is passing,' answered Virginia, stepping to the window and drawing up the
blind. It was true the clouds were lifting, and under their dark canopy there
lay along the horizon an ever-widening line
of light. ' But you are tired, Emmeline. I
will leave you for the present ;' and she
went out into the hall, followed by Jack.
' Where is Aunt Charlotte ?' she asked, as
she paused there irresolute.

' In her bed-room, I believe. She thinks
it weak-minded to be frightened, so she
always hides herself when there is a storm.

She had Marshall with her just now, and he must still be somewhere in the house. He was afraid to go away.'

The girl made no answer but walked on till she reached the library door, and opened it slowly. A man was seated at Mr. Stansfield's writing-table reading a letter, which he dropped as he rose and turned to her with a hasty bow and muttered greeting.

'Good-evening,' answered Virginia, slightly inclining her head. Then, stooping to pick up the paper: 'You have dropped a letter, Mr. Marshall.'

She stood confronting him with it in her hand. It was addressed to Norton Stansfield.

'There must be some mistake,' she observed, still with her steady eyes upon him. 'This letter is Mr. Stansfield's.'

'And you were reading it,' cried Jack, in high falsetto; 'yes, you were, Mr. Marshall, I saw you. Since when has Norton made you his private secretary? What does he pay you for answering his letters?' giving the discomfited steward a push with his elbow.

'I can hardly be expected to reply to—to impertinent insinuations,' stammered Marshall. 'I was delayed by the violence of the storm, and having some business to transact . . .'

'You varied your occupation with some lighter reading,' cried the irrepressible Jack.

'Jack, be silent,' exclaimed Virginia. She walked to the writing-table, lit a taper, and sealed the letter which she still held. 'I shall give this to Mr. Stansfield, Mr. Marshall, when he comes in this evening, and tell him under what circumstances it came into my hands.'

'If you would allow me to explain . . .'

'You can make your explanations to Mr. Stansfield,' answered the girl, coldly; and she moved towards the door.

Jack, forbidden to vent his wit upon the steward, had already beaten a retreat, and gone off to harry the maids in the cellar.

'Stay one moment,' exclaimed Marshall, directly placing himself in her way. 'If you do not hear what I have to say, you may be sorry for it afterwards. I have no wish to make use of my knowledge. I have no desire to injure you or any other young lady. I will never repeat what has come to my knowledge, if you on your part will undertake to intercede for me with Mr. Norton.'

'I can have nothing to say to you, Mr. Marshall. Be good enough to let me pass. I do not understand your meaning.'

'Then you may understand it one of these fine days, and to your cost,' muttered the man, as the door closed upon her. 'I have not after all kept watch here for nothing. Even Stansfield may be glad to buy me off.'

In the meantime Virginia, as she mounted the stairs, had soon dismissed him from her mind. She had dreaded this return to the scene of her misfortunes. She had shrunk from the sight of the bed on which she had passed so many sleepless nights of bitter weeping, of the garden paths about which she had wandered in restless misery, of the spot where the death-warrant had been read out to her; yet now, even in this first hour, a calm had fallen upon her spirits. Mr. Stansfield had been right. She was glad that his roof should shelter her; here, though she might not find a home, she would yet feel that she was not a stranger.

A door opened and Mrs. Stansfield came to meet her.

'My dear Virginia, what weather for you to arrive in! But we are very glad to have you amongst us once more;' and she drew her into her bed-room. Mrs. Stansfield's room was, like herself, orderly and methodical. From the folds of her bed-curtains to the row of slippers beneath the dressing-table, everything was in its place. One felt that one ought to apologise to the chairs for sitting down upon them lest one should rumple the chintzes. Perhaps some feeling of the sort oppressed Virginia, for she responded somewhat shyly to her aunt's greeting. 'Yes,' continued Mrs. Stansfield, 'Emmeline and I shall be really grateful for your company. This house has not been a pleasant habitation of late: Norton has had one of his moods upon him. One cannot but pity those who have to live with him under those circumstances, and Emmeline, poor girl, is little fitted to withstand tyranny. Certainly his behaviour might shake stronger nerves than hers. I confess I am selfishly glad that he is out on this your first evening.'

'Is he away?' asked the girl, colouring a little.

She was conscious of a sense of dis-

appointment.   He had made such a point
of her return to his house, she could not
but be surprised that he had not cared to
be there to receive her.

'Yes, he is not coming back until to-
morrow, perhaps not even then.   Possibly
he thought that you would rather be
alone with me and Emmeline on your first
arrival.'

Then he had expected her! and Virginia knew well that the excuse his step-
mother had advanced would never have
entered his mind.   She sat down by
her aunt's side, and looked somewhat
thoughtful.

'Perhaps you are not aware that Norton has in a measure constituted himself your guardian,' continued Mrs. Stansfield.   'Mr. Everard, for some unaccountable reason, refuses to act, but the matter
must be looked into.   I cannot say that I
feel satisfied, but a woman is so helpless;
when Hartley is once more in England I

shall have some one to act for me, and then . . .'

'I shall in all probability not be here,' interrupted Virginia, quickly. 'By that time I should hope that my affairs may be arranged, and that I need be no farther trouble to anybody.'

'I hope that you will not talk of being a trouble. My dear child, you are too young to be left to yourself; you must look upon Stansfield as your home.'

'It is very good of you,' answered Virginia, in a low voice, 'but . . . but I could not do that always; yet for the present I shall be very glad if I may stay with you.'

'I wish that it were my house so that I might say stay with us always;' and Mrs. Stansfield took one of the girl's hands in hers, 'but it is difficult to feel oneself mistress in a house where Norton is the master, and he is so intractable. Really, your presence in the house need make no difference to him.'

'Does it make any difference?' asked Virginia, raising her head quickly.

'Emmeline is right, my dear child, you ask very inconvenient questions, and you must not look upon this as a personal matter. He has always been morose and disliked women's society. The mere fact of a stranger in the house sends him into that state of reserve with which it is so difficult to deal.'

Virginia looked somewhat discomfited for a moment, but she could not help remembering that the reserve which Mr. Stansfield had manifested towards her had not been marked, and certainly he had shown no distaste for her society. She did not, however, contest the matter with her aunt. In one respect the facts were against her : Norton had not cared to be at home to meet her that evening.

She went along the passage to her own rooms with lagging footsteps ; through a window to the west the sun poured in a

stormy radiance of vaporous light; she
could hear Jack whistling in the distance,
but she no longer experienced the sense
of rest and security which had been hers
an hour ago. Even here there were
jealousies and deceptions, and her only
friend had failed her.

'No! I must not stay. I must go away
as soon as possible with Mademoiselle
Joseph. She at least is faithful,' she said
to herself; and she sighed, for though, as
she had said, the world is wide it is melancholy to wander alone through it in search
of a resting-place, and sorrow had robbed her
of her courage, and for the time the spirit of
enterprise had died within her. She went
on into her bed-room and throwing herself
upon the bed laid her face on the pillows
and burst into a passion of tears. 'If only
he could come back for one day, one hour,'
she sobbed in her ignorance, as she kissed
over and over again her father's miniature.
How he had always cared for and guarded

her. How difficult, how impossible life seemed to be without him!

She had still a dull despair at her heart when she awoke the next morning to find the June sunshine flooding a transfigured world. It spread a golden mist over the fair pastures and dewy lanes, and the young leaves tossed their glittering freshness against a cloudless sky. Virginia had wandered out alone; from force of habit she had sought the walled-in kitchen garden where wallflowers and raspberry canes grew in close proximity and the air was sweet with thyme and lavender. No one was to be seen but an old gardener nailing up the fruit-trees; it was a still and sunny enclosure sheltered from the wind. Virginia walked to a corner where the light foliage of an acacia spread itself above a bench, and sat down leaning her head upon her hands. She was oppressed at heart, weary of her life. She had known, it is true, a sharper grief, a more poignant sorrow, but

never before had such a dull and hopeless
apathy weighed down her spirits. A bird
spread its wings against the heavens and
trilled its gay song above her head, the
butterflies flitted amongst the young cur-
rant-bushes, even the old labourer croon-
ed a methodist hymn, and still she paid
no heed, but sat with bowed head and sad
eyes fixed upon the ground.

' Have you come home already?' asked
a voice at her elbow. Mr. Stansfield was
standing before her. Unmistakeable pleasure shone in his dark eyes as with outstretched hand he drew her to his side.
' So you have come home.'

She had risen startled at his approach
and coloured beneath his scrutinizing gaze,
conscious that the signs of recent tears
could not well escape his keen observation.

' Is it too soon?' she asked, laughing a
little in confusion.

' Yes, since I was not here. What right
had you to steal a march upon me in this

way. How could I think that you would leave Hinton before eleven. I know that breakfast there is never early.'

'I breakfasted, however, at Stansfield,' answered Virginia, 'for the very good reason that I also slept there last night.'

'You came here yesterday?'

'Why does that surprise you? Certainly I came here yesterday in spite of the storm. I have a prejudice in favour of keeping my engagements, and that day had long been fixed for my arrival.'

'Yet Mrs. Stansfield mentioned the 22nd. I am sure of it, and to-day is the 22nd, Wednesday the 22nd. I suppose,' drily, 'she was not at all astonished to see you.'

'She concealed it very well,' answered the girl, quick as usual to catch his meaning. 'She was even kind enough to explain the reason of your absence.'

'As to which you probably felt no curiosity?'

She hesitated for an instant; and then she said, frankly,

'Yes, I did. I thought that you would have been here.'

'Nothing, but this misunderstanding would have kept me away,' he answered, hastily, whilst his eyes gave a quick response to hers. 'How will you make up to me now for the time that I have lost?'

'Oh, it was not all wasted,' said Virginia, smiling. 'I have learnt more about you than I might have done if you had been at home. I have had a full description of your character.'

'This becomes interesting,' he said; but he looked a little uneasy. 'It is useful to see ourselves, so moralists tell us, with other people's eyes; will you not help me to know myself?'

Virginia had seated herself once more upon the bench. She was twisting a spray of laburnum in her fingers, like golden flies its blossoms lay upon her black dress, on which the swaying acacia boughs spread a shifting net-work of light and shade. Her eyes were cast down; an uncertain smile hovered about her mouth.

'You are gloomy,' she said, softly, 'gloomy, morose, and a tyrant. It is your own fault, if I am rude. Are you afraid of the truth?'

'Go on,' he answered, grimly. 'Do not be afraid of hurting my feelings. Let me hear the rest.'

'You dislike women; so I am not to mind, it is not any personal animosity which makes you object to my presence here at Stansfield.' She spoke sedately enough, yet the colour deepened in her cheeks, and she would not look up at him.

'Mrs. Stansfield told you that I objected to your presence here?' he cried, angrily. Then, more calmly: 'She is not worth one's anger. She should have selected some less palpable falsehood. You surely, surely,' a little anxiously, 'did not believe her?'

'I did not think that she was right, and yet . . . I have always been accustomed to believe what I am told . . . and you were not there,' answered Virginia, deprecatingly.

'Then you can have no faith in the absent;' and his brow clouded. 'Can you then be said to have any faith at all?'

'I don't know,' she said, and drooped her head. 'I think I have lost faith in everything lately. Perhaps you are right.'

'Why, what perversity is this?' he continued. 'Did I not come myself to ask you; nay, more, as your guardian to insist upon your coming back? You know— you know that I wish to have you here; even if,' in a low voice, 'even if you know nothing else.'

'I am glad to know it,' she said, simply. 'You need not be angry with me for a natural, a momentary doubt. I am glad to come back.'

The June sunshine was reflected in her eyes, blue and clear as the summer sky. She had risen, and the golden blossoms lay scattered at her feet; her brown head was uncovered, her hands were lightly clasped together.

'Then stay,' he said, looking down at her.

'But, Mr. Stansfield . . .'

'Will you never give me another name?' he interrupted.

'Why, you yourself forbade it,' cried the girl, laughing. 'Have you forgotten the time when you were so anxious to prove to me that we were not cousins?'

'That relationship is not necessary. Do none but cousins call each other by their Christian names?'

'I cannot tell you,' answered Virginia,

shaking her head, 'but perhaps when I know you better, some day—some day I will call you Norton—to vex Mrs. Stansfield.'

CHAPTER V.

'Do not let anyone know that it is my
birthday, Mademoiselle Joseph,' said Virginia. 'Oh,' sighing, 'how I used to love
my birthdays.'

'My poor child,' cried Mademoiselle
Joseph, wiping her eyes.

It was a lovely morning. Virginia
stood upon the balcony of their little
sitting-room, leaning her arms upon the
balustrade. Below there lay the flower-
garden, with its smooth lawn and brilliant beds of geraniums and lobelia,
symmetrical and gaudy, and yet, in their
setting of dewy turf, with a certain jewel-
like beauty of their own; on the steps of
the terrace a peacock spread his gay

plumage, and the fountain played amongst the roses. The air was full of undertone, the whisper of leaves, and the low hum of insects.

'Do not give way, my darling, do not,' said Mademoiselle Joseph.

'Do I give way?' asked the girl, with a melancholy smile. 'I did not think I could be accused of that. Do I not eat and drink and sleep just as I used to do, and sometimes I hate myself for it. If I had died instead,' bitterly, 'he would never have got over it.'

'But when one is young wounds heal more easily,' answered the governess, giving utterance to the very truth against which the girl was so passionately rebelling. 'Besides, you know, he never wished, he never could have wished you to grieve. It is not true to say that you are not altered. I have sorrowed for you, my poor child.'

Virginia did not answer; she hardly

heard her. Over and over again in mournful retrospect she recalls the words and gestures, the looks, the very tones of her beloved dead, all those nameless trifles which constitute an individuality; she trembles lest longingly, as she recalls them, they may be obliterated by time; she strives after them already, even as through the dark we strive to discern the lineaments of a familiar face.

'Virginia,' Jack cries from below, 'I am going to fish. If you will come with me, you may put on the worms.'

But she shakes her head, and declines this tempting invitation.

'Mr. Stansfield has sent to ask if he may come up,' says Mademoiselle Joseph, presently. 'He wishes to see you or me. May he come up?'

'If he likes,' she answers, indifferently. 'Last year,' she is saying to herself, 'only last year.' There is a dull mist before her eyes, the geraniums shine and burn through it like little tongues of flame. 'Why did I let those precious hours go by so quickly?' she is thinking; 'why did not I draw from them even a deeper draught of happiness? why did I not lavish upon him a greater wealth of love?'

'May I come in?' asked Mr. Stansfield's voice at the door.

'Certainly, come in, monsieur,' and Mademoiselle Joseph rose to offer him her chair in which she was sitting. She had had little opportunity to forget whilst at Stansfield that she was a dependent and a stranger. But Norton would not be seated, he passed on to the balcony and stood looking down for an instant at the girl's bent head and dejected figure.

'Will you come out with me this afternoon?' he asked.

'No, I think not. Why this afternoon?'

'Why not?'

'Because I am not very good company to-day,' she answered, trying to smile. 'You would not find it at all amusing.'

'I think that I could manage to dispense with amusement for one afternoon. And I want to drive you over to Hinton. Lady Mainwaring has never forgiven me for taking you away, and I should like to make my peace with her; and in the afternoon when the sun is not so hot the drive would do you good.'

She shook her head. 'I think that I would rather not go out to-day.'

'Not to please me?' he pleaded, with a sudden change of tone.

'Would it please you?' she asked, looking astonished.

'Not if you do not like it.' A cloud had come over his face; a cloud of annoyance at her sincere and evident surprise.

'But I do like to please you, Mr. Stansfield;' and she laid her hand upon his sleeve. 'I have not the chance to please many people, and I do not find it easy to please myself. I will go with you to Hinton, it was only that this afternoon...'

'You were thinking of other 26ths of June. Yes, I know it; but that is one reason why I want you to come with me to-day.'

'Who told you that it was my birthday?' cried Virginia. 'I hoped that nobody would know it. You must promise, promise not to tell Mrs. Stansfield or Emmeline.'

'I swear it,' he replied. Then, rather shyly: 'Do you remember once telling me that you liked presents? I—I have brought you a little present.'

'Oh, how very kind of you,' cried Virginia, flushing.

He took from its wrappings and held out to her a small chased vinaigrette of curious and elaborate workmanship. Her fingers touched his lightly as she took it from him and surveyed it with manifest gratification.

'How pretty it is!' she said, with a child's sincere pleasure.

'Yes, it is a quaint little thing. It took my fancy and I hoped that you would like it.'

'I like it very much.'

Mr. Stansfield's answering smile bespoke even deeper gratification as he watched the little hands busy about the clasp and fastenings of his gift. 'Some day,' he was thinking, 'she may be ready to accept something else at my hands.'

They did not go to Hinton after all. There was a distant farm which Norton had long wished to visit, and he proposed to take this opportunity.

Virginia had no objections to offer. She was fond of Lady Mainwaring, but upon this special afternoon she felt no wish for her society. The long lonely drive which Norton proposed suited her better, and it was not till the afternoon was well advanced that he came to summon her. In fact he had first waited to see his step-mother and Em-meline drive off in the barouche to return the calls of some country neighbours. He had no desire to keep his expedition a secret, at the same time he wished to avoid comments and possible opposition.

Mrs. Stansfield had sedulously tried to keep Virginia apart from him; and was but partially aware of her ill-success.

It is late when after a long drive across some unfamiliar country and by unknown byways they turn their faces homeward. The clouds are gathering in the west and the sky is darkening. They will hardly reach home in time for the eight o'clock dinner. Norton has begun to feel uneasy. He is aware that she may in consequence be subjected to a cross-examination from her aunt, and he dreads anything which may disturb her calm or shake her childlike confidence.

It adds to his dismay to find that his

horse is going lame, and to discover, when he gets down to investigate the cause, that he has dropped a shoe. It is of little avail to anathematise the carelessness of the groom, who is safe from his wrath in the stables at Stansfield, and in silence he considers the length of the way and the changing sky.

'If only one saw a cottage or could find a blacksmith,' he ejaculated, looking up and down the lonely road and across the untrodden fields.

'Does it matter so much?' asked Virginia, who sat in the pony-cart with some wild-flowers in her lap. 'I am in no great hurry to get home. Are you?'

'I feel no irresistible desire to be once more in Mrs. Stansfield's and Emmeline's company, if that is what you mean. But we cannot well walk home, and Toby,' touching the cob's sleek coat, 'will hardly take us there.'

'And you will miss your dinner,' observed Virginia, looking a little dismayed in her turn. ' Wait,' standing up in the pony-cart, ' I believe I see a house, which looks like a farm not very far off across those fields.'

She is right, and in a quarter-of-an-hour they arrive at it. The farmer himself is away, but his wife, a little meek and melancholy woman in a silk dress and a gold chain, asks them to come in whilst one of the men takes Toby to the nearest blacksmith. Norton paces up and down the front garden and Virginia is shown into the parlour. The blinds are all down, and there is a faint musty odour as of long stored fruit. Mrs. Bryce, the farmer's wife, takes an inquisitorial survey of Miss Tennant's dress and looks and figure, whilst in a dismal monotone she delivers gloomy prognostications as to the weather.

Virginia paid no heed to her; she felt a little weary, a little depressed, but no forebodings as to coming storms

or the lateness of the hour and the darkness of the way had power to disturb
her tranquillity. When the pony-cart was
brought round, and Norton came in search
of her, she rose with alacrity. Mr. Stansfield, on the contrary, looked decidedly
out of humour, and frowned as he glanced
at the old-fashioned clock in the corner.

'Have you no wrap or shawl of any sort?'
he asked. 'I fear it will rain. Mrs. Bryce,
can you lend Miss Tennant something?'
And, in spite of her remonstrances, he
wrapped the girl closely in the plaid which
the farmer's wife brought forth.

'But you are smothering me,' cried Virginia.

'Never mind,' he answered, shortly,
putting her into the pony-cart. 'Mrs.
Bryce, is there no shorter way than that by
which we came? We shall be very late if
we go round by the road. There surely
used to be a bridle-path through Langley
wood.'

'Yes, and there was a path still wide
enough for carts,' so Mrs. Bryce assured
them, ' certainly it would be three miles
nearer to return that way to Stansfield,
but then there was the ford by Langley
church, and sometimes it was impassable ;
still she believed that she had seen some
one who had come that way to-day. Yes,
certainly, it must have been that morning
Joe Gibson had crossed it.'

Mr. Stansfield thanked her, looked once
more at the darkening sky, and turned
Toby's head in that direction.

The grass lay cut in fragrant ridges in
the fields and its faint clean odour was
borne upon the freshness of the evening
air. The high hedges were hung with
clematis and starred with pale dog-roses;
every now and then a flash of summer
lightning broke on the ripples of the grey
sky like moonlight on the crest of a wave.
Soon under cover of the woods the heavens
were altogether lost to sight and they

drove more slowly along the narrow way; every now and then a branch cracked above their heads as they grazed the trunk of a tree by the wayside.

'Are you afraid?' asked Norton, suddenly bending towards the girl whose face he could not even attempt to read by the uncertain light.

'No, I am not at all afraid,' answered Virginia, cheerfully. 'I do not very much like the dark when I am by myself, but to-night I have you and Toby to keep me company, and besides I do not think I could ever be afraid in a wood : so many innocent things have their home here. Soft-coated squirrels and rabbits and woodsprites who are always supposed to be a quiet harmless race of people. I think it is very beautiful here under the trees.'

But even as she spoke they were emerging once more into open ground, and after crossing a strip of common turned into the narrow lane leading to the ford. To their left the river rushed by some old farm buildings in a fall of foam across the weir, though upon the other side of the bridge the current widened and flowed calmly through the level fields. In the light of the rising moon the mass of river daisies upon its breast gleamed like a silver shield. For an instant, Norton drew the reins and from the quiet landscape turned his eyes upon the girl's fair delicate face.

' Is it still beautiful ?' he asked, smiling.

' Yes, very beautiful.'

' And you have been a little happy to-day ?'

' 'I have had a happy afternoon, yes, thank you, Mr. Stansfield.'

' Do not thank me,' he answered, shortly, touching the pony with the whip. Then, as they drove on along the narrow lane : ' I wish that it were light enough to see if there are recent marks of wheels upon this road.'

'Have you already forgotten Joe Gibson?'

asked Virginia, laughing. 'If he passed
through, surely we may do the same.'

It is very still in the little hollow
through which the stream has made its
way; they can dimly discern the square
outline of the old church on the other side,
but the great yew-trees which surround it
are black and shapeless masses against
the sky; the water, however, as Mr. Stansfield perceives to his dismay, is higher than
he has seen it before, and Toby has hardly
stepped into it when he plants his forefeet
firmly and refuses to proceed. It is in
vain to urge and coax him on, and when
Mr. Stansfield is proceeding to stronger
measures Virginia lays a detaining hand
upon his arm and implores him not 'to hit
him.'

Norton's answer is to lift her from the
pony-cart, and under the shelter of the
hedge she hears sounds of a conflict
and the splash of the water. But in a
short time Mr. Stansfield comes back.

He is vexed, though laughing. Toby is hot, dripping, but the conqueror.

'I am afraid it is no use. It seems impossible to get you over this evening. I am afraid that Toby is right.'

'In spite of Joe Gibson,' cried Virginia, provokingly. 'I thought that what Joe Gibson had done Mr. Stansfield could surely do.'

'It seems you were wrong!' answered Norton, who was decidedly out of temper. 'Unless that fool of a woman made a mistake. She has sent us so far out of our way now that we shall have to go miles back to get into the other road.'

'I am afraid you do not bear up well under adverse circumstances;' and Virginia laughed a little softly. 'Confess that you would not mind it so much . . .'

'If you were not here,' interrupted Norton. 'Yes,' gravely, 'that is quite true. Are you warm enough?'

'I am much too hot muffled in this

great shawl, if that will restore your good temper. I was going to say that you would not mind it so much if you did not want your dinner. I feel for you, I am not cold, but I am rather hungry.'

'Poor child!' he said, and quickened Toby's pace.

Nevertheless, the moon was already high in the heavens, and the threatening clouds in which the sun had set had given way to the clear pallor of night, before they drew up under the portico at Stansfield.

'You are very tired?' he said, glancing at her face as he lifted her down.

'A little tired,' she answered, smiling, as the clock in the stable-yard struck eleven. 'I must go to Mademoiselle Joseph. I fear she may have been uneasy; so good-night.'

But there was no uneasiness in her own voice. No fear of misconstruction or of possible reproofs in store for her had for an instant crossed her mind.

'Stay for a moment.' Then, as she turned upon the step in obedience to his call: 'I think you had better not go to your aunt to-night. I will explain our late return.'

She gave a careless assent and went on into the hall.

'Oh! my dearest child, what alarm you have occasioned us,' cried Mademoiselle Joseph. 'What apprehensions, what fears!'

'Which were quite groundless,' answered Virginia, kissing her. 'We have had a series of mishaps but no adventure worth recording. I will tell you about it when I have had something to eat.'

'But your aunt wished to see you immediately upon your return. I dare not let you delay. She is in her dressing-room.'

'Where I cannot go to her,' cried Virginia, rebelliously. 'I am dead-tired, hungry, and sleepy. It was Mr. Stansfield's fault that we were so late. He must make my apologies.'

'But she is already in her dressing-room, my dear Virginia.'

'Which is an additional reason why I should stay away. Depend upon it, dear mademoiselle, she would not have retired to her bed-room at this hour unless she had some object in view. I suspect that she wished to scold me for disregard of her dinner-hour when Mr. Stansfield was not by to take up my defence. Punctuality is her god, but as it is the first time I have transgressed, I do not feel very guilty, and if there is a scolding in store I prefer that Mr. Stansfield should bear the brunt of it.'

They had reached their own sitting-room, and Virginia had taken off her hat and shawl and was leaning back comfortably in the depths of a great arm-chair whilst she watched Mademoiselle Joseph draw out a little table and arrange upon it the supper that she had kept in readiness.

'This is much better than being scolded,' she cried, gaily, surveying the preparations with satisfaction.

'Virginia,' cried Jack, putting in his rough flaxen head at the door. 'Let me come in. I am so glad you are not lost or drowned. Let me come in to drink your health, Virginia.'

CHAPTER VI.

Mrs. Stansfield was seated stiff and upright in a high-backed chair, and Virginia
was standing before her; but the severity
of her aunt's gaze was wasted upon the
girl whose attitude was by no means that
of a culprit. Her eyes were straying out
of the window across the sunshiny lawn to
the patch of shade under the chestnut
where Jack lying upon his face with his
heels in the air was whistling cheerfully a
tune which like a piping bull-finch's
always broke off in the middle.

'I am really sorry to speak, Virginia, but
what can I do? You would not wish me
to allow you, no doubt ignorantly, to
expose yourself to disagreeable comments,

and I confess that I was annoyed yesterday evening, very much annoyed.'

'I am very sorry, Aunt Charlotte,' answered Virginia, not however very penitently. 'I know that you like people to be punctual, but you see it was not my fault that Toby dropped a shoe and that the rains had swollen the river, and please remember that I have hardly ever been late before.'

'If it were only being late for dinner!'

Mrs. Stansfield looked graver than before, and sighed as she folded her hands slowly together.

'Why, what else have I done?' asked Virginia, opening her blue eyes in sincere surprise.

'Is it possible that you do not know?'

'It is not only possible, it is quite certain that I do not know what you mean, Aunt Charlotte.'

'Some girls have instincts!' murmured Mrs. Stansfield. 'It should not be neces-

sary to give commands about these matters.
But it is true your bringing-up has been
unfortunate, that is your excuse. Yet I
should have thought that even you might
have known that an excursion such as you
saw fit to take yesterday, alone with a man
against whom your best friends had warned you, was neither fitting nor proper. I did
not wish to have to say this, Virginia, I
hoped your own feelings, your instincts
would have been a sufficient safeguard.'

The girl stood still and silent for a
moment, with deepening colour and a
mingled expression of surprise, anger, and
bewilderment upon her changing countenance, and then she said, a little proudly,

'I have not, it is true, been accustomed
to think that I needed any safeguards, nor
do I need them now against Mr. Stansfield.'

'You are mistaken in him, Virginia. I
have told you so before. You are an
ignorant girl and he is a man of the world.
He would not scruple at anything which

served his own ends; he would not reflect that you might be compromised.'

'Was it his fault that the pony was lame and the river unfordable?' cried Virginia, impatiently.

'Was it so impossible to drive home earlier and by another road?' asked Mrs. Stansfield, fixing her inquisitorial glance upon her.

'You mean that he purposely made our drive longer and missed his dinner only that he might get me in to a scrape? Perhaps it is because he wants you to send me away,' cried Virginia, with some lurking laughter about the corners of her mouth. 'You know you told me last week that he found it irksome to have me here. Well! he might have got rid of me in some simpler way.'

'Dear Virginia!' exclaimed Mrs. Stansfield, a good deal relieved by the girl's unconsciousness, and beginning to perceive that reproofs were worse than useless. 'I believe I need say no more. You are a good child and will remember what is due to me and to yourself. Be a little more careful in the future, and remember that Norton is not Hartley.'

' I am not likely to forget it,' thought Virginia, as she walked away into the garden. 'Certainly Hartley and Mr. Stansfield have nothing but their surname in common.'

No suspicion of past indiscretion upon her own part disturbed her spirits. Her aunt's insinuations had glanced harmlessly aside, and she walked bare-headed in the sunshine with a mind as unclouded as the midsummer sky. She looked surprised when at the corner of a shrubbery walk she met Mr. Stansfield and Mademoiselle Joseph in close conversation, and saw that Norton looked grave and a little uneasy, whilst the poor governess's flushed cheeks and disordered appearance betrayed some inward agitation.

'What is the matter?' cried Virginia. 'I hope, mademoiselle, that you are scolding Mr. Stansfield. I have had more than my share of blame, and I should like to transfer it to some one else.'

'Then suppose that we send for Toby,' answered Mr. Stansfield. 'Or, if we are to go back to the final cause, to the groom who looks after him. I cannot, however, find it in my heart to be very angry with either of them.'

'Nor I,' she answered, lightly. 'It was a lovely evening in spite of Mrs. Bryce's prognostications. At the same time I do not like being scolded, and I have been scolded this morning.'

'By Mrs. Stansfield? And why?'

'Why? For no very good reason an-swered" the girl, evasively.

'I should, however, like to know it. Tell me what she said to you.'

Virginia drew back to Mademoiselle

Joseph's side. Possibly she shrank a little from the tone of authority.

'Perhaps I would rather not tell you, Mr. Stansfield.'

'Nevertheless you will,' he answered, smiling. She coloured a little and gave him an answering smile though she still hesitated.

'Well!' she said, 'Aunt Charlotte thought that I had forgotten that you were not Hartley. That was a mistake, I had not forgotten it.'

'No! What else did she say?'

'Nothing that I minded very much. She only thought it right to put me on my guard against you.'

'You did not mind that?'

'Not in the least,' cried Virginia, laughing. 'I was to take care that you did not make the pony lame and lose your way home another time, and neither of these things are likely to happen again. It was not my fault, was it?'

'If you please, sir, Mr. Marshall wishes
to know if he can see you.' A footman
had brought the message, and now stood
waiting for an answer.

'Yes, tell him to wait;' and Mr. Stansfield was turning again to Virginia when
he perceived that a change had come over
her. She looked confused, penitent, and
altogether disconcerted.

'That detestable man. I had forgotten
him until this minute. Mr. Stansfield,
will you ever forgive me? I have had a
letter of yours which I took from him days
ago and never remembered it until now;'
and she related in a few words the scene
in the library.

'Oh, how could you have interfered at
all in the matter, my dear Virginia!' cried
Mademoiselle Joseph. 'He has a spiteful
disposition. He will be certain, in some
way or other, to revenge himself upon
you.'

'And may I ask where my letter is at

this moment?' inquired Mr. Stansfield, rather shortly.

' I think . . . I believe it must be still in the pocket of my jacket ;' and, for once, Virginia looked decidedly abashed. ' I have not worn it since the day I arrived. I will go and look for it.'

' Let me go, my dear child,' cried Made-moiselle Joseph, who was always willing to run everyone's errands. ' I will find it and bring it here.'

' No, indeed, I will go myself ;' and Virginia, rather anxious to escape from Mr. Stansfield's grave eyes, in which she read some displeasure, was turning away when his hand upon her wrist detained her.

' Indeed, if Mademoiselle Joseph will be so kind, you shall stay here.'

' If I *please*,' observed Virginia, with some emphasis and heightened colour as he released her from his momentary clasp, seating herself upon a bench at a little distance.

'Certainly, if you please,' he repeated.
'But I think you will acknowledge that a
little curiosity upon my part as to this
letter which you have seen fit to withhold
from me is not unnatural. Can you remember the look of the envelope? It was
not a blue one, was it,' rather anxiously,
'addressed in a bold, round hand with
initials in the corner?'

'Yes, I believe that it was. I am
almost sure there were initials. H. E. or
F. E., I think.'

Mr. Stansfield did not speak, but he
looked decidedly serious.

'Was it anything of importance?' asked
Virginia. 'Yes, I see that it was. I am
very sorry.'

'It is of no consequence, unless that
scoundrel has read it.'

'But he did. I am afraid that he did.
He did not deny it. Mr. Stansfield, I am
really very sorry that I kept your letter.'

'My property could not be in better

hands,' he answered, rather stiffly. 'As to Marshall, I ought to be able to deal with him. Say nothing of this to your aunt, Virginia.'

It struck her that it was the first time he had called her by her name; she thought, a little resentfully, that it had escaped him unawares, it was a matter of no consequence, he had not remarked it. He walked away across the lawn to meet Mademoiselle Joseph; she saw him take something from her, and then pass on into the house.

She got up restlessly, and walked to meet Mademoiselle Joseph.

'What were you talking to Mr. Stansfield about just now?' she asked, putting her arm in the old lady's.

'Nothing, nothing that you need be troubled about, my dear Virginia.'

'But I am troubled already. I hate all these mysteries. You can have no secrets from me. What can Mr. Stansfield have said to you which I may not know?'

'I did not say that he had said any-thing.'

'No, but you cannot deny it, and, be-sides, you looked guilty. I saw it at once when I joined you.'

'If you wished to know what Mr. Stans-field was speaking of, you had better have asked him,' answered Mademoiselle Joseph, with some asperity, driven to this unusual tone by the difficulties of the case.

'You know very well that it would not have been of the slightest use. I have generally been able to get other people to do as I wished; but Mr. Stansfield treats me as . . . as a child;' and she petulantly kicked away a pebble.

'Nevertheless, lately I have begun to believe that you were right and that he is indeed your best friend.'

'I do not know,' answered the girl, rather sadly. 'I have undergone a good many disillusionments of late. I do not feel very sure of anything, Mademoiselle Joseph. Even you,' returning with the persistency of a child to the forbidden subject; 'even you have your secrets.'

'Oh, my dear Virginia, it is not my wish,' cried her perplexed guardian. 'I said from the first that I wished to have no concealments; but now what am I to do? I have given my promise to Mr. Stansfield, and——'

'And I will not ask you to break it.' Virginia looked up; her good temper, which was rarely ruffled, was restored; and she was sorry for Mademoiselle Joseph's evident distress. 'If it is really Mr. Stansfield's counsel that you are keeping, it can be no affair of mine.'

'Oh, dear, dear!' sighed the poor governess, truthful and perplexed.

'Come, let us think of it no more,' cried Virginia. 'I am afraid that I have already unwittingly done Mr. Stansfield an unkindness. I will in return forgive him for

having made you his confidante. Go in
and rest, mademoiselle; you look tired.
I shall stay out for a while. I do not wish
to encounter Mr. Marshall.'

And so she walked on alone, but her
cheerfulness left her with Mademoiselle
Joseph. She had no wish to add to the
troubles and perplexities of her old friend,
but she was experiencing in herself that
cruellest of disenchantments, that loss of
confidence in those whom she had trusted.
Even Mademoiselle Joseph had her secrets;
and she did not understand Mr. Stansfield.
It was very true, as she had said, she no
longer felt sure of anything; the ground
was slipping away beneath her feet.

'Oh, Virginia,' cried Jack, meeting her
as she was returning to the house, 'you
have got us all into a nice scrape this time.
You really should not walk off with other
people's letters; in these matters, as I have
always told you, you cannot be too careful.
But why, *when you had read it*, did you not

give the letter back to Norton, which would have saved all this bother ?'

'When I had read it ?' cried Virginia, aghast.

'Yes, when you had read it ; it need not surely have taken you a week to do that.'

'Do not be such a torment,' cried the girl, angrily. 'You know perfectly well that I should not have read Mr. Stansfield's letter.'

'No, you should not. You are quite right there; but what a pity it is that we never think of what we should or should not have done until it is too late. I have no doubt,' consolingly, 'that the temptation was strong. Better people than you have given way before. I might even have done it myself; and if Norton can forgive you . . .'

'He knows that he has nothing to forgive.'

She was too much perturbed to take Jack's assaults cheerfully; depressed and ill at ease, she was in no humour for *badinage*.

' Well! he has no real right to be angry, since the letter concerned you, and you alone.'

' How do you know that?' cried Virginia, taken off her guard, and betrayed into instantaneous and natural curiosity.

' I did not think it right to leave Norton undefended,' answered Jack. ' So, during his interview with Marshall, I stationed myself beneath the library-window, where I distinctly heard my proud elder brother desiring, or, indeed, asking Mr. Marshall not to divulge to Mrs. Stansfield the knowledge he had obtained by so unscrupulously reading a letter which concerned Miss Tennant. Yes, Virginia, I heard your name distinctly. I am speaking the truth now, as if I were upon my death-bed; for I cannot see why Norton should constitute himself the sole arbiter of your fate. I would not allow it, if I were you.'

She turned aside to break off the stalk
of a geranium; the colour of the flower
was reflected in her cheeks, tears of vexation
had gathered in her eyes.

'It is not I that allow it . . . it is
because . . . because I am so alone.'

'Why, Virginia! Not when you have
me,' cried Jack, really sorry to have vexed
her, rubbing his flaxen head against her
shoulder.

'It is impossible,' continued Virginia,
after a moment's reflection, slipping her
hand into his, a little comforted by his
demonstration. 'It is quite impossible that
Mr. Stansfield should have any secrets
about me, and with Marshall.'

'But you must remember it was Marshall
who thrust himself into it. Certainly
Norton is anxious it should go no further.
He said that great annoyance would result
to . . .'

'Stay!' cried Virginia. 'I have heard

too much already. You had no right to listen.'

'Nonsense, Virginia; all is fair in love and war, and it is war; war to the knife between me and Marshall. If Norton will not buy him off, he will do some one a mischief; and Norton will not care, he never does care for anyone but himself.'

'I do not believe that, neither do you in your heart, Jack,' she answered. 'But I will ask Mr. Stansfield.'

She stopped, and hesitated, remembering that it would be of little avail to put any questions to him which he did not wish to answer.

'No, no, leave it to me,' cried Jack. 'Since you are so scrupulous, I will not listen again at doors or windows, but I will just keep my ears open. Some day I may hear of something to your advantage, Virginia.'

But the girl only sighed. It did not

seem to her that any good was laid up for
her in the future. She had left it behind
in the coffers of the past, to which she had
lost the key.

CHAPTER VII.

'I NEVER was more surprised in my life!'

The observation came from Mrs. Stansfield. She did not often allow herself to feel, far less to betray, any astonishment. It was an emotion unbefitting the mistress of a household and the mother of a family, but for once she was taken off her guard.

'It is inconceivable,' she cried, beginning to walk restlessly up and down the room. 'I believe now that Norton knew it from the first, and concealed it from me. I never could have believed that Reginald would have been so foolish. He was not a man to look after his own interests, I knew he was careless about money; but then his income was sufficient to cover small extravagancies. Still, to have left his money to be invested by Mr. Everard! It was culpable negligence. It is most unfortunate.'

'It might have been much worse,' observed Emmeline, who, from the sofa, was contemplating her mother's disturbance of mind with languid curiosity. ' Remember, if you had had your way, she might have been your daughter-in-law.'

'A girl without a penny!' ejaculated Mrs. Stansfield. 'Yes, that would have been a misfortune indeed.'

' Poor Virginia !' said Emmeline, softly. She was genuinely sorry for her. To her, poverty was an unmixed evil. It meant hard fare, and flock mattresses, and cold mutton. 'It would kill me,' said Miss Stansfield to herself. Yes, she had felt for Virginia when, pale and dejected, with that inexplicable change upon her which comes to those who for the first time have met with death, she came out once more amongst them from her chamber of sickness and despair; she had felt for her as one feels for a grief of which one has had no experience; but this was another matter.

Emmeline understood what it would be to lose all these comforts of daily life which were to her necessities. She had at times been forced by some accidental circumstances to forego one or another of them, and she had suffered. Fortunately Virginia had been differently brought up, but still it was very hard upon her.

'She is very pretty, but no one would marry a penniless girl, and mamma will not want to keep her here,' thought Miss Stansfield, easily divining her mother's intentions.

'What can she do?' she asked, aloud.

'I shall have no objection to her remaining here for a few weeks,' answered Mrs. Stansfield, magnanimously. 'But, you see, with Hartley coming home before very long, it is impossible for me to keep her. I always said it was a difficulty with Norton on one side and Hartley on the other.'

'Hartley who was to fall in love with her, and would not, and Norton with whom she was not to fall in love. Well, mamma, you have certainly escaped from one danger, and I do not think that you have fallen into the other.'

'No,' answered Mrs. Stansfield, composedly. 'At one time I was a little uneasy. But Virginia is evidently heart-whole, and Norton looks upon her as a child. I have been speaking to him about her to-day, and he has behaved very well upon one or two points, though, as I said, I believe he would have kept this from me even now, unless Marshall had seen Mr. Everard's letter, and come to me about it.'

'It is going rather far even for Marshall to read other people's letters,' observed Miss Stansfield. 'What are you going to do about it?'

'Well, that is one point upon which Norton has behaved well. He does not urge me to take any immediate measures, which would be very inconvenient, and he sees my position. He has not taken up Virginia's side in any quixotic spirit, as I feared that he might. He sees that she must go, and he has only made one request, which is that I will tell her nothing until he has seen Mr. Everard once more. There may be some alleviations, though I hardly think it likely.'

' Oh, how I should hate to be poor! Poor Virginia!' sighed Miss Stansfield, again reaching out her hand for her smelling-bottle.

In the meantime, Virginia herself was in silence maturing her plans. She felt it impossible to remain at Stansfield. Her aunt's manner perplexed her; it was at once patronising, chilling, and compassionate. She no longer even took the trouble to reprove her; she was indifferent as to her occupations, she asked no questions, she did not seek her society. More than ever the girl lived her life apart; and yet Emmeline was kind, kinder than she had ever been before; only she, too, seemed at times embarrassed, as if she hardly knew what to say or to leave unsaid.

' It is very clear,' thought Virginia, with a slight touch of bitterness, ' they all wish me away, but they do not like to say it openly. I wish Mr. Stansfield would come back. I do not like to leave without wishing him good-bye, but I have now nothing else to wait for.'

Mr. Stansfield's absence was, however, protracted beyond the appointed time, and Mrs. Stansfield only received a long letter from him, which she read and pondered by herself. He did not enter into details, but he assured her that business arrangements could not be completed for a month. He pledged himself to see that by that time everything should be arranged,

and Miss Tennant and Mademoiselle Joseph
should leave Stansfield 'in a manner to
cause no inconvenience nor discomfort to
anyone;' but on the other hand, if he
undertook the business, he required upon
Mrs. Stansfield's part a promise that Virginia should until that time arrived know
nothing of her altered circumstances. He
must, he said, insist upon this guarantee
if he were to fulfil his part of the agree-
ment.

Mrs. Stansfield was puzzled; but, though
ready to suspect, she could see none but
obvious and justifiable motives for his
request. Men always hated any disturbance of the domestic atmosphere, and, if
Virginia during her last weeks at Stansfield took her reverse of fortune to heart,
it might be very unpleasant for everybody;
she would be really, for the first time in
her life, grateful to her stepson if he could
save something out of the wreck, so that
the girl might naturally slip away into

retirement without awakening any comments. Mrs. Stansfield had no wish to
earn an undeserved character for harshness or want of feeling. It would be far
better if no opening were to be given for
ill-natured criticism; yet nevertheless she
hesitated before giving a distinct promise;
circumstances might arise to make it ad-
visable to enlighten Virginia, and Mrs.
Stansfield prided herself upon being a
woman of her word. She had a great
respect for it; her own unwritten precepts
were as binding as the moral law. Still it
was a choice of evils, and, having taken a
day for reflection, she wrote to her step-
son :

'I cannot perceive the reason of the
condition you exact, but I shall be thank-
ful if you can arrange this very trying
business, and, as you desire it, I will say
nothing to Virginia until the month has
expired.'

Norton received the letter just as he

was starting for Stansfield. He did not take it out of its envelope until he found himself alone in the railway carriage ; and then, though he cast his eye rapidly over the pages, those were the only lines that he cared to read. He had at least disarmed one enemy; ' but what will that avail,' he said to himself, ' if she herself is against me ?' and he looked out thoughtfully over the country as, in a shifting panorama of wood and pasture and upland, it was spread before him. Virginia did not love him—not yet ; and what he had to do must be done so quickly. Gloomy, morose, and a tyrant, this was what they had told her of him ; and yet she liked him, but with that frank, childlike liking which is so far removed from love. She must be left free ; there must not be even the slightest appearance of constraint; she must never know (not, at least, until he had won her) that, but for him, she would be homeless.

He had dined in town, and it was past
nine o'clock when he turned in at his own
gates, and, telling the man to drive round
with his luggage to the stable-yard, walked
slowly up the approach.

It was a still night.   Overhead the stars
shone faintly in a dusky sky.   The air
was clear and soft, the day had drawn
gently, almost imperceptibly, to a close,
and night was as quietly stealing into its
place.   Under the grey heavens, sur-
rounded by its woods and dewy pastures,
the old house seemed more than ever the
abode of peace.   Here, if anywhere on
earth, wounds might have time to heal,
and passions should be stilled. ￮ Mr. Stansfield felt himself to be in harmony with the
place, and with the hour: he loved this
girl, tenaciously, it is true, but yet calmly
almost dispassionately, as one loves when
the first illusions of life have been dis-
pelled, and when the season of passion is
over.

He was in no haste to enter the lighted drawing-room, where he would find his step-mother and Emmeline sitting with closed shutters; he had no wish to meet Virginia in their company; he would prefer to wait until the morning, when he might see her alone; and, lighting a cigar, he was turning into a side-walk, when a sound of rustling leaves and of something moving near arrested him. It was only Ponto, the old house-dog, but he was sniffing the ground according to the promptings of his social instincts, which always sent him upon the track of any member of the household who might be abroad, and Mr. Stansfield, following his footsteps down an over-grown shrubbery walk, came in a few moments upon the object of his search.

A low stone wall bounded upon this side a miniature rose-garden, and against this wall Virginia was leaning. By the faint and shadowy light he saw the outline of her slight figure; and caught the unconscious grace of her attitude, as, resting her head upon her hand, she looked out over the darkening landscape, but she did not move at his approach, not even when he uttered her name.

'I hope that I did not startle you.'

She murmured a negative, but her words were almost inaudible, and she made no movement, she did not even turn her head in answer to his greeting.

'Are you not anxious to hear how your business has prospered?' he continued. 'I have seen Mr. Everard, and as you wished,' (smiling), 'I have brought you some money.'

Still no answer, only a slight movement of her head showed that she had heard him.

'What have I done?' But he waited in vain for a reply. 'What have I done? What has happened since I went away that now upon my return you will not

even speak to me? Look at me, Virginia.'

And then at last she slowly and reluc-
tantly turns her face towards him. Even
by the dim starlight he can see that she is
deadly pale; the dark lines beneath her
eyes tell of long weeping, and her sorrow-
ful blue eyes are even now dim with
tears; she makes an effort to speak, but
the words die upon her lips; and, once
more turning from him, she hides her face
in her hands.

He too is absolutely dumb, silenced
by new and overpowering emotions. Only
a quarter-of-an-hour before, looking back
upon the dark days of his past, his
love for Virginia had been to him as
a breath of spring air, as a gleam of
sunshine. What, then, was this stormy
light which had broken upon his soul,
shattering the old beliefs and pierc-
ing the shadows? Even pity itself is
drowned in a flood of sweet and bitter

revelations. She is so near and yet so far removed from him in her absolute unconsciousness and the abandonment of her grief.

The moon shining through a mist touches the rough stones upon the wall, and the fine tendrils of the creepers twined about it are sprays of silver; but the girl's brown head is still in shadow, though the moonlight trembles in the folds of her dress, and glancing across her shoulder shows her bare rounded arm and throat beneath its transparent texture.

'It is not anything that you have done,' she said, after a few moments, 'it is only that I am ashamed to be so unhappy.'

'Not ashamed before me?'

'Yes, especially before you, who have done your best, who have taken so much trouble to help me. Especially before you, who would console me if you could.'

'Can I not console you?' He dares say

no more; but there is a vibration in his voice which startles her.

'Oh, yes,' she cries, quickly. 'You do console me. Your goodness consoles me. Still . . .'

'Yes, still—tell me, what did you mean to say?'

'Still I am like a sick person whose pain you cannot relieve; like a beggar whose hunger you cannot satisfy; sympathy consoles us for evils, but cannot cure them.'

He does not contradict her. He only says,

'Will you tell me your troubles?'

'You will not think them very great,' she says, smiling mournfully. The moon now shines full upon her pale face, and even the lovely curves about her mouth and the rounded cheeks look as if they were fashioned out of marble. 'You will despise me. I despise myself. It is not only that he is dead,' and she shivers a little, ' but I want so much that he used to give me. I was always flattered and spoilt and admired ; it was like the sunshine, I could not live without it. I was not selfish,' apologetically, 'I wanted other people to have it too; but I loved to be loved.' She breaks off suddenly with rising tears.

' And now !' His breath comes quickly as he asks the question, and he averts his eyes from her.

' Now if I say more you will think that I complain, but you can see for yourself that I have no place here. Aunt Charlotte is anxious for me to be gone. And Emmeline is kind, but I do not amuse her any longer. Then I thought that Mademoiselle Joseph at least would be glad to come with me to France, and even she seems changed. Yes, I know I am very foolish, I ought not to mind so much. But it is as I have told you. I have been spoilt.'

'And so you came out to cry alone in the moonlight. That was not a very wise proceeding, was it?'

He speaks gently, but she turns away and makes no answer. It was true, as she had said to Mademoiselle Joseph, he treated her as a child. She is sorry now that she has spoken to him.

'Are you offended?' he asks, after a pause. 'Well!' smiling a little, in spite of his concern at her obstinate silence. 'You have told me your story. Shall I tell you mine? You say that the sunshine has gone out of your life, do you know when it came into mine? It had not been too full of affection. Stansfield was my home. I had certain rights which could not be put aside, but I too was not wanted here. My life was full of occupation, but it was very lonely. You know, you have told me before, that I am moody and bad-tempered. I suppose there is a certain truth underlying most misconceptions.'

'I only repeated Aunt Charlotte's words,' interrupts Virginia. 'I did not believe it.'

'No, and it was very foolish of you, you had no grounds for your unbelief, but you did not believe her; and I knew it. I knew that it would be so even from the first time that you pushed open the library door and broke in upon my solitude. I disliked interruptions. I wondered at your audacity, but yet I was glad of it.'

He stops abruptly, and she turns her eager, questioning gaze upon him. Surprise and a dawning pleasure have dried up her tears.

'Yes,' he continues, 'you do not know how glad. You do not know what your smile and your little outstretched hand was to me. How it has changed this old house, and altered the whole aspect of life.'

He breaks off in deepening perplexity. Like a gathering cloud, it obscures his rising hope. He knows well enough that she cannot understand. The chord which he would have touched is not broken but as yet unstrung.

'I did not know that you liked me so much.' She smiles at him in the moonlight. His words have brought no faintest touch of colour to her cheeks. 'Was it,' a little curiously, 'was it from the very first?'

'Yes,' he answers, a little unsteadily, 'from the very first.'

'How long ago it seems,' she says, sighing a little. 'Only ten months, and it seems like ten years!'

In spite of his self-control, he turns from her with a quick movement of half-resentful pain.

'Because you are weary of your life here? Because you are tired of Stansfield?'

'No, not that. It is because so much has happened; one life has ended here, and I must begin another; and I dread it. It is very cowardly, I never used to be afraid, but I am afraid to go away alone.' Her voice has sunk almost to a whisper. Before them the long line of undulating ground, broken here and there by clumps of twisted thorn and birches, lies outspread in the misty moonlight. Virginia rests one hand upon the rough stone-work, the other hangs down listlessly at her side. She looks very young and fair, a lonely little figure looking out into an unknown world.

'Virginia,' he says, and he has put so strong a restraint upon himself that though the words have leaped to his lips he speaks quietly, 'you shall never go away if you will stay with me.'

She is startled at last. The colour flushes in her cheeks as she turns towards him, and even yet she cannot, she does not understand. How is it possible that she should be still so unconscious of the passion which is mastering him; and yet that very unconsciousness has laid, as it were, a seal

upon his lips. The prince, as he entered
the palace, must have waited for a moment
upon his knees before he gave the kiss
which should awaken his sleeping love.
She will never rest so lightly and so peace-
fully in her father's halls again.

'How can I stay?' she says, rather
tremulously.

'You must trust me altogether,' he
answers, 'that is all. See, Virginia, it
is a great deal that I ask; I know it, and
yet I ask it. Will you marry me?'

There is a long silence. He will not
hurry her; neither by word nor look will he
break down that shield of delicate reserve
which is her natural defence. He will
conquer, but it shall be with honourable
weapons; and so he waits, though his
mouth is firmly set and he is paler than
usual.

'Can you give me an answer?' he says,
at last breaking the silence.

'No,' she answers, and her voice is

now clear though low, ' I cannot. I told
you just now that I was afraid. Well, I
should be afraid of that.'

' What! afraid of me ?'

' No, not exactly ;' and she smiles a
little. ' You have been very good to me.
I have never been afraid of you. But you
are asking me to go away with you into an
unknown country. I . . I do not like new
things. I do not wish to be married.'

' Virginia,' he says, so gently that the
words hardly sound like a protestation,
' I would give all the years of my life to
make you happy, and think them well
spent.'

' Do you really care for me so much !'
She stretches out both her hands towards
him ; the magical moonlight encircles her
head ; her mouth trembles into a smile, but
the tears are running down her cheeks.

' So much ! God knows, my little sweet-
heart !' he cries. ' God knows.'

His dark eyes look down into the blue

depths of hers. For the moment he has forgotten everything except his love. Far off a clock is striking the hour; a light wind rustles and shivers in the trees; old Ponto lying at their feet rises and stretches himself; and like a stormy cloud darkening the clear surface of a pool he sees his passion reflected in her troubled eyes. He drops her hands and stands a little apart.

' Would it make you happy if I married you ?' she asks, softly, as if perplexed.

' Yes,' he answers, hoarsely. He can utter but the one word. It seemed as if at this supreme moment of his life his heart stood still, and the confused landscape, like a tempest-tossed sea, rose and wavered before his eyes.

' Then I will.' And she drew closer to him, and with a sigh and a smile slipped her little cold hand into his.

CHAPTER VIII.

'I only ask you to keep your promise,' said Mr. Stansfield. He stood leaning one elbow upon the drawing-room chimney-piece looking down at his step-mother, who, flushed, angry, and uneasy, sat upon an ottoman close beside him. 'Ten days more and you will be released from your pledge. I might have asked for a longer respite, but I am aware that it would be of no avail. I might have appealed to your forbearance towards one as lonely and friendless as Virginia, but I knew that it would be useless. But for the next ten days, remember, that you have given me a promise.'

'You would do well to release me from it,' she answered, gloomily. 'You think it best to keep Virginia in ignorance of her true position. It will be all the worse for you when the truth can be no longer concealed.'

'I will take the risk,' he answered; but no assurance of victory lighted up his face. It was a risk, and he knew it; but if Virginia were once his wife Mrs. Stansfield might do her worst. Till then at any rate she should believe that she did not come to him penniless; till then she should not know that but for him she would have been homeless and alone. No one should dare to tell her that pity or generosity had mingled with his love.

'But in ten days what will you gain?' asked Mrs. Stansfield.

'There is no possible reason for delay,' he answered, quickly. 'We need no great preparations; the circumstances of the case, her mourning, and Mademoiselle

Joseph's illness will all necessitate a quiet wedding. You need give yourself no trouble about it.'

'You mean to be marriedat once?' Mrs. Stansfield's voice was raised in horrified and genuine surprise, and she rose from her chair in excitement. 'And Virginia has given her consent to this indecent haste? Well, you have not asked my advice, but I must tell you to ease my own conscience that I consider your conduct perfectly unjustifiable, and, yet more, disgraceful.'

'What is the matter?' asked Virginia, who with some flowers in her hands was at that moment entering the room through the open window. She had caught Mrs. Stansfield's last words, and now pushing aside the muslin curtain she looked enquiringly from her to Norton.

'Mrs. Stansfield has an uneasy conscience, that is all,' he answered, quietly enough, though his countenance betrayed some discomposure. 'Stay,' as he saw his step-mother about to speak. 'If you desire it, I myself will tell Virginia the reason of your displeasure, though,' with a sudden flush of colour, 'I had not thought to tell her thus without preparation and in your presence. Virginia, Mrs. Stansfield is angry because I want you to trust yourself to me now, at once.'

'How, when?' asked the girl. She was a little startled but still uncomprehending. She came forward and rested one hand upon the table on which she had laid down her flowers. 'What do you mean?'

'He means that he wants to *marry* you at once,' cried Mrs. Stansfield, with bitter emphasis and gathering rage. 'You, a child with no knowledge of the world, with no due sense of what you are doing. Yes, I know you have never asked my advice, you have thought me prejudiced, but does not this at least prove that I was right. What man with any sense of what was fitting, or even knowing what was due to yourself, would make such a proposition ?'

Virginia had turned a little pale, but she gave no other sign that she was moved. She would not even look at her aunt. Her torrent of anger had to all appearance spent itself in vain; like a wave which frets itself against a rock. And Norton only looked at Virginia.

' Your aunt's words, more than anything else, prove that I am right,' he said. ' You must let me take you away as soon as possible. Believe me,' gently, ' I am very sorry to hurry your decision.'

' Sorry !' and Mrs. Stansfield's voice rose to a high *crescendo*. 'Have you no shame, no consideration for a young girl who knows no better ? Her inexperience may be some excuse for her, but have you no thought of what the world will say ? Yes, listen at least to what I have to say ;' she perceived that she had over-reached her mark, and moderated her tone a little. Norton's darkening countenance showed that he would not listen in silence much longer, and Virginia's small teeth were firmly set, and her hand tightly clasped over a jewelled paper-knife she had taken from the table. 'You may as well listen for this once. If you are to be married, allow her at least a proper time for consideration; and I for my part will not oppose, though I may lament the arrangement. In six months' time, if you still hold to it, she shall be married from this house as if she were my own child. She has trusted you blindly, do not abuse her trust.'

But Mrs. Stansfield's appeal made no more impression upon her step-son than her anger. A half-contemptuous smile just touched his lips and passed, leaving him as grave as before. Mrs. Stansfield turned to Virginia.

'I have warned you,' she cried, shrilly. 'I told you before that he would deceive you. He is deceiving you now, and you

L 2

will find it out sooner or later, and then
you will remember my words, when it is
too late.'

'It is too late already,' said the girl;
and with a swift movement she crossed
the room. She stood before Norton, and
looked up at him; her eyes were full of
burning indignant tears. 'Why do you
let her say such things?' she cried. 'I will
not listen.'

'And you will do as I wish?' He looked
down into her flushed, upturned face.

'It shall be . . . as you please.'

She caught her breath a little but she
never turned her sweet, direct glance from
his. He kissed the little hands he held,
and then he said: 'Come out into the
garden;' and drew her to the window. He
knew well that, bravely as she had borne
herself, her heart was beating fast and she
was trembling in every limb. But he said
nothing until they had reached the stone
seat by the fountain, where thick-growing

cypresses and laurels made a green and shaded solitude. Then she sank down on the low seat, and, for the first time since her father's death, burst into passionate sobs and tears.

'It is so cruel of her! I was beginning to be happy. I have no one but you, and she would poison it all.'

'But she cannot,' he answered.

He sat down beside her, and she clasped her hands round his arm and laid her head down upon them. She was very lonely, shaken by past sorrow, unnerved and desolate, and, as she had said, she had no one but him. A great tenderness arose in his heart to still the passion of his love. If only here, in this little green corner of the world, he, whose life had been so often empty of joy, might rest in its full completeness. He bent and kissed the soft, brown hair upon her brow.

She stirred a little uneasily and lifted her head.

'And the worst of it is that she is right,' she said, and the tears were still wet upon her cheeks. 'It is too soon. I would not own it to her, but do you think that I do not feel it? I should like to wait, I should like to be free a little longer.'

'And yet you trust me?'

He dares not put another question; he dares not ask her if she loves him, for too well he knows the answer.

'Yes; always,' she said, with a sigh, and put her soft fingers upon his sleeve. 'I always did. As you told me, it was very foolish.'

'Then believe me now. There are good reasons for what I ask, or I would not ask it. You may see some of them for yourself. You shall not be exposed any longer than I can help it to Mrs. Stansfield's insults. It is intolerable to me not to be able to defend you even under my own roof, and we cannot ask her to leave at a week's notice. When we return she will be gone, and Stansfield,' very gladly, 'will be our home.'

'I like Stansfield,' she answered, brushing away her tears. 'I like this sheltered garden and the shrubberies, and the house with its long passages and sunny window-seats. I like no place so well except La Vallière.'

'Do not make me jealous of La Vallière, where I never knew you;' and he smiled. 'Some day we will revisit it together.'

Then there is silence again between them except for the dripping of the fountain and soft cooing of the pigeons in a distant dove-cote.

'And when shall it be?' he asked, after a little while.

He spoke very gently. Perhaps he felt the loneliness of her position at this crisis of her life even more than she felt it herself. Other girls had their mothers to care for them, and sisters and friends; a home circle of which, for the time, the one

about to leave it was the one absorbing
object of interest.   There, in an atmosphere of affection which was a sort of
pledge and guarantee of greater love to
come, a young girl's misgivings would be
quieted, and she would step out encouraged
and supported from the old world to the
new.   But Virginia had nothing to sustain
her but poor Mademoiselle Joseph's nervous fidelity.   And the old Frenchwoman
was very feeble in mind and body.   For
the last week she had been very failing.
She had no hope to put before Virginia,
only a faint satisfaction in the thought
that she would no longer be her sole
protector.

'When shall it be?' he repeated.

The girl awoke with a start to the
present from a dream of other days.   The
mention of La Vallière had taken her back
into the enchanted land of childhood.
She thought of the little green arbour
where she had set out her childish feasts;

of her bed in the old nursery, with its muslin curtains, through which many a time she had looked out, with a child's awestruck curiosity, at the spangled, starry heaven; from whence, on winters' nights, when the curtains were drawn, she had watched strange, shadowy shapes flitting in the firelight across the walls. She thought of the little patch of violets under the window, which she had planted and watered; of the church with its tinsel shrine and painted altar, like the court of heaven. She saw herself once more a child, in a white pinafore, running to meet her father at the gate. How real it seemed! Then Norton's voice recalled her to the present, and she was sitting beside him in a strange land, and the old, familiar things had vanished once more into the dim shadows of the past, and he was asking her when she would marry him!

'When?' she echoed, shrinking back a little. 'Oh, I . . . I do not know.'

'Shall it be to-day week; next Tues-day?'

He retained his self-possession only by an effort; but he had advanced too far to retreat, and it was an absolute necessity for him to obtain an answer to his question. Virginia started up, and walked away a few paces. He made no movement to detain her; he only followed her with his eyes. She stood by the fountain, and its light spray was tossed above her head, but her downward look was fixed upon the dark surface of the pool, upon which the leaves of the water-lilies lay outspread. He could not tell whether he had angered or only frightened her. Even to himself his proposal came as a shock; as she had said, it was very soon. For a few weeks only had he even called her by her Christian name. A few months ago he did not know that he loved her; she did not even now know that she loved him. Yes, she was right. It was cruel of him to ask it, and

yet it was a necessity, an absolute necessity to win her consent.

He waited for a while, and then he rose
and stepped to her side.

'You have not given me my answer,
Virginia.'

'Because I do not know what to say;'
and she lifted her troubled glance to his.
'I do not want to be unkind. I know you
have been very good to me . . . but I do
not think that you understand.'

'Then help me,' he answered, smiling
rather gravely. 'Tell me what it is that
you fear.'

'It is because it is all strange and unfamiliar,' she answered. She had sat down
upon the edge of the fountain, and was
drawing her fingers mechanically through
the water. 'I am not afraid here alone
with you in this old garden. I am happy,
I could be happy, if you would not talk
about the future. You are my friend, and
I am very friendless but for you. I like

to talk to you, it interests me. I should like a share in your business as well as in your leisure. I am not afraid of you, even when your eyes grow black and you are angry. Your step-mother said you were like a thunder-cloud. Well, you know that I like a storm. It exhilarates me.'

'Go on,' he said, as she paused for a moment. 'So far I understand you.'

But to himself he said, if she loved me even a little, she would not speak so freely.

'But I do not like new things, I told you so before,' continued Virginia, 'and I *hate* promises.'

'What promises? Yes, you shall tell me,' taking her hand, and drawing her round so as to face him. 'What promises?' and his glance, smiling yet imperative, demanded an answer.

'All promises;' and she drew her hand away and turned her head aside, vexed to feel that she was reddening beneath his scrutiny. 'And it is for always;' and her

voice sank to a whisper. ' Till death . . .
It frightens me.'

' Would not you be more afraid without
me ?' he answered. ' It is not so very long
ago, is it, that you told me the world was
empty and you were alone. Virginia,' his
voice suddenly softening, ' will you not let
me take care of you?'

' I like you to take care of me,' she
smiled ; and, drawing her hand from the
water, lightly shook the drops from it and
held it out to him. ' So if it can only be in
one way . . .'

' It can only be in one way,' he answered,
seriously, pressing her little fingers fast in
his.

' Well, I am willing.' Then very con-
tentedly. ' What a firm clasp you have.
I like it. It gives me courage.'

He cannot answer. He is only conscious
of an overmastering impulse which it takes
all the strength that he possesses to resist.
Since he cannot awaken an echo to his

love he must, at all hazards, preserve her unconscious confidence in him. It is his only chance.

'Then I shall tell Mrs. Stansfield that it is to be on Tuesday.'

'Tell her what you please,' answered Virginia, who, now that this point was settled, was regaining her spirits. 'Only do not let her be angry with me if you can help it. I do not like to be scolded. I am very sorry that she does not like me, and I know that I have been a trouble to her, but it will not be for much longer, and it has not been altogether my fault.'

'We need not trouble her at all if you are willing.' And then he paused. He dreaded to touch upon even the most necessary details lest they should bring the fact upon which they depended more vividly before her. She was idly balancing herself now upon the stone coping of the gravel walk. In spite of past sorrow, she looked very young and careless; it was no wonder that she was reluctant to relinquish her freedom. 'We are going to be married,' he said, smiling, 'but you will be content, will you not,' hesitating a little, ' without a wedding ?'

'No one is to be there but Mademoiselle Joseph,' cried the girl, with a sudden flush of colour. ' I will not have anyone invited. Promise me that it shall be as I wish, Mr. Stansfield.'

' Is that a command or a request ?' Then, bending his penetrating gaze upon her half-averted face: 'Cannot you word it differently ?'

' Promise me, Norton.' She drew closer to him, and spoke softly with her eyes upon the ground.

'So you will have no bridesmaids, no favours, no wedding-cake ?' he asked, half-laughing.

' No, and I will have nobody there but you and Mademoiselle Joseph,'she persisted, ' and Aunt Charlotte and Emmeline of course if they choose to come. It must be quite early in the morning.'

'Why quite early in the morning?' He had dreaded to bring any details before her, and now her words struck a chill upon his heart. These anticipations bewildered him; he would rather, far rather have had any amount of girlish shrinking and shy fears to contend with. He was staggered by her very confidence in him. 'Why should it be so early?'

'The world looks best when it is first awake,' answered Virginia. 'Besides,' more seriously, 'I shall not have so much time to be frightened. Ah,' seeing the cloud which had come over his face, 'you need not be angry; and it is no use, for you cannot frighten me. It is all very well for Aunt Charlotte to say that you are deceiving me, but I know that it is not true. You were good to me even from the first day that I came into the house, when I was nothing to you, not even a cousin, only a friendless, lonely little girl, an uninvited guest and a stranger, and now I know that you liked me even from the first, and I . . .'

'Yes, and you?' he echoes, with a sudden irrepressible desire to hear his sentence from her own lips.

'I liked you; I like you very much, Norton.'

'Better than anyone else?' he asks, in a rough, shaken voice. What madness impels him that he cannot forbear to question her, that with most unwise scrutiny he seeks an answer in her face?

'Yes, now better than anyone that is left to me,' she answers, sighing, as she thinks of the love of her life of which she has been for ever bereft.

'Better even than Mademoiselle Joseph?' with rather a bitter laugh.

'Yes, it is very ungrateful of me, better even than Mademoiselle Joseph.' And she too laughs a little, but softly. 'Poor

Mademoiselle Joseph, I have left her alone too long. I must go in;' and she began to walk towards the house.

Norton did not offer to accompany her. Her slight figure, in its black draperies, passed from under the shadows and across the patch of sunlit grass. He remained behind looking gloomily down at the fountain.

CHAPTER IX.

For the last ten days Mademoiselle Joseph
had been very ailing. There was a crushed
look about her figure, a gentle melancholy
in her speech. Sometimes it seemed to
her that life was too heavy a burden to
be borne, but she had a sensitive horror
of laying it down lest anyone else should
feel it their duty to take it up. She sat
unoccupied in her chair, with nerveless
fingers folded together upon her lap, and
started and guiltily took up her book or
her knitting when anyone came into the
room. And yet at first she would not
own that anything was the matter with
her. She had the greatest dread of being

M 2

a trouble or inconvenience to the household; it distressed her beyond measure to
have the housemaid asked to bring her up
a cup of tea, and it was with many faltering excuses that she confessed herself
unable to come down to dinner.

Then Virginia took alarm, and the
doctor was sent for, but he was a rough-
and-ready country practitioner, and, as he
could give no definite name to her malady,
he considered that there was nothing very
much amiss. Perhaps he was right in one
sense, the machinery was in order, but
nevertheless the clock was running down,
and its beats were slow and faint. Poor
Mademoiselle Joseph! so much had been
required of her, and she had only one
virtue, fidelity; so she said to herself,
sitting dull and silent in her stiff arm-
chair.

When Virginia came in, she looked at
her with a palpable and pathetic effort at
cheerfulness as she asked some trivial

question; but the girl did not answer it. She came and knelt down by her side instead and laid her head upon her shoulder.

'Have you been lonely? Have I left you too long?' she asked, softly.

'No, no,' cried the old lady, nervously. 'You must never fancy that, my dear child. You have been with Mr. Stansfield. That is all as it should be. You must never let him think that I take you away from him.'

'He need not begrudge me to you;' then she gently passed her hand up and down the folds of Mademoiselle Joseph's dress, and said, in a slightly altered tone, 'I am going to marry him on Tuesday.'

'On Tuesday. Oh! my dear Virginia!' She let her hands fall with a gesture of terror, almost of despair.

'But there is nothing terrible in that,' cried the girl. 'And if you are not better we will not be married at all. You must not fancy that I would leave you.'

'Oh, dear, how little you know what you are saying,' sighed her faithful guardian. 'What is this little attack of illness of mine in comparison with this supreme moment of your life. Oh! Virginia, I have prayed, I have hoped it may be for the best. You must not let any misgivings of mine disturb you.'

Virginia raised her head, and with a little quick movement shook back a loosened wave of hair from her brow.

'Why should I be afraid?' she asked, smiling. 'It is true that, as I told him just now, it is soon, very soon. But nevertheless he is right. Aunt Charlotte will be glad when we are gone; and you will not be solitary; you are to go to Lady Mainwaring's until we return; she wishes it.'

'She is very kind, but it was not of myself that I was thinking.'

'No! when did you ever think of yourself,' asked the girl, fondly. 'But you

must not be unhappy about me, mademoiselle. See ! what could I desire more ?
He is well able to take care of me; he
is strong and kind; and,' in rather a
lower voice, 'he loves me, Mademoiselle
Joseph.'

'But you,' cried the old lady, with irrepressible anxiety, 'what of you ?'

'How fond people are of asking questions,' answered Virginia, rather petulantly. 'You are as bad as Mr. Stansfield.
Have I not told you before that I like
him. I like him very much. I trust
him entirely, he has never deceived me.
I am glad to go away with him.'

She walked to the window, and, after an
instant's pause, stepped out on to the
balcony. Yes, for the moment she was
tired of Stansfield. The shadow of past
sorrow hung over its sunny lawns ; there
was a coldness and estranged embarrass-
ment in her intercourse with its inhabi-
tants; she had but little in common with

her aunt or Emmeline, and she was impatient to escape. Even Norton was graver and more preoccupied than usual; and poor Mademoiselle Joseph's weakness made her fretful. Virginia was very patient with her, but her youth rebelled against her fears and lamentations. 'I could be happy,' she thought, 'if Mademoiselle Joseph would not sigh over me and Norton would not ask questions.' After all, she was very ignorant, and she did not imagine that she had anything else to fear.

Emmeline could have told her otherwise, but a complication of motives kept her silent. She was really sorry for Virginia, and shrank from a warning which would give her possibly useless pain; then she detested the worry of domestic scenes, and as she would have said did not feel equal to the emergency. Perhaps, as she said to herself, after all her mother might be right to put every obstacle in her power in the way of this undesired marriage.

'Only remember, mamma,' she observed, fretfully. 'I will not be used as a stumbling-stone. I should be trodden upon or kicked out of the way, and I should not like it.'

'Is it any great hardship, then, to leave Stansfield for a few weeks?' answered Mrs. Stansfield. 'I shall make all arrangements. You need only leave yourself in my hands. Believe me, Emmeline, it is the truest kindness to Virginia to prevent this hasty marriage.'

Two mornings later, Virginia, leisurely descending the stairs after breakfasting in her own rooms with Mademoiselle Joseph, was surprised to see portmanteaus and packages in the hall and her aunt in a large travelling-cloak superintending the preparations.

'What has happened, Aunt Charlotte?'

'A sudden summons which I cannot

refuse. My poor sister-in-law is taken worse at Torquay. We can only reach her by leaving at once. I received the letter by the early post, and I take Emmeline with me. The change will do her good, and she will be a comfort to her cousins. I was coming to tell you, but have been so hurried. Yes, the dress-box is quite light, and will go on top of the brougham, Mason. Ask Miss Stansfield if she is ready.'

Virginia stood silent, somewhat suspiciously noting the elaborate preparations; the neatly-strapped shawls, the travelling-bag in the hand of Martin, the lady's-maid, the sufficiency of luggage.

' I have no time to discuss any plans with you now, Virginia,' continued Mrs. Stansfield, hastily packing some sandwiches into a basket. ' I will, of course, write to you at once.'

The girl made no answer; she went on

into the dining-room, where Emmeline was finishing her breakfast.

'It is so miserably early for a journey,' she grumbled. 'I never can eat at this hour of the day, and we shall not be at Torquay till the evening. It is a horrible journey, but mamma will insist upon my going with her.'

'For whose sake, I wonder?' asked Virginia, a little scornfully.

'Emmeline, Emmeline!' her mother was calling. 'If we miss this train there is not another for three hours.'

Miss Stansfield rose hastily, and approached her cousin.

'Good-bye, Virginia. It is not my fault.' For an instant she looked into the girl's blue eyes, at that moment rather sad and cold. 'Be wise; you are too good for Norton,' she said, and kissed her. But Virginia made no response. She followed her into the hall, and saw the brougham drive away, with the dress-box on the top of it, and her aunt and Emmeline inside, and then she went slowly back into the empty drawing-room.

'So this is Aunt Charlotte's last device! It is not kind of her;' and hot tears sprang to her eyes. In a minute or two she brushed them away with a laugh. 'Why should I care? It is only that one does not like to know that some one wishes to injure you. But why should I regret her departure? It is much pleasanter here without her and Emmeline. But still I know that she thought I should mind. I do not believe she intends to return by next Tuesday. I must go and console poor Mademoiselle Joseph.'

But, as she turned to leave the room, Norton entered it. He glanced at her somewhat apprehensively, and looked relieved at her smile.

'Egypt was glad at their departing,' cried Virginia; the morning sunshine fell upon her slight young figure, and its light was reflected in her eyes. 'Do you realize the fact that we are in disgrace, too bad even to be scolded? I remember it happened to me once before when I was a little girl. I was shut up in an empty room; I was meant to be a prey to the pangs of conscience, but instead of that a little mouse came out of a hole and played with me. I remember it perfectly. I was very happy.'

He smiled a little, but still somewhat uneasily. Only that morning he had casually heard of his step-mother's departure and had been at no loss to discover a motive for her precipitate retreat. It was her last move. She would at all hazards render his immediate marriage with Virginia impossible. She had no compunction in exposing the motherless girl under her care to possible or even certain misconstruction.

Norton's face darkened as he thought

of it, and Virginia, suddenly looking up at him, asked with incredulous surprise,

'Is it possible that you are unhappy at Aunt Charlotte's and Emmeline's departure?'

'I am a little puzzled,' he answered.

He had advanced to the table and stood leaning his hand upon it. His glance rested calmly and thoughtfully upon Virginia. If he had once lost the mastery over himself, at least he had not been slow to regain it.

'When do you imagine that she will come back?' he inquired.

'Why should we so soon begin to think of that evil day?' and she looked up and laughed in his face. 'The sun is shining, and for this week at least we shall have Stansfield to ourselves.'

But her absolute unconcern only served to deepen his perplexity. She was, as she said, so alone in the world, and, deprived of her natural protectors, she had no one

but him to care for her. Her very ignorance increased his responsibility; and
anger against his step-mother, who had of
set purpose placed her in a difficult position, was of little avail, since she had passed
beyond his reach.

'Yes, we shall have Stansfield to ourselves,' repeated Virginia, lightly, walking
to the window and leaning her graceful
head out into the sunshine. 'I shall do
all the things that have been most strictly
forbidden. I shall pick the flowers in the
conservatories; and invite the dogs into
the drawing-room. I shall go in the punt
on the river and pick water-lilies; oh, how
I wish that Jack had not gone back to
school.'

'Shall not I do as well?' asked Norton,
smiling at last, in spite of his unsolved
perplexities. She had been so often sad
and serious of late that he could not but
be glad to see her once more, if only for
an hour, careless and light-hearted. 'I

cannot send for Jack, but I will do my best.'

'Then come, let us go down to the river,' cried Virginia, holding out her hand to him.

But all through the sunny morning hours, even with her bright eyes looking up at him, and her little hand in his, he remained somewhat grave and thoughtful. When they returned to the house, luncheon was laid in the dining-room, but there were no signs of Mademoiselle Joseph. Virginia went up to seek her, and came back again in a few minutes to say that she would rather not come downstairs. The heat of the day had tired her, and she was resting. But she was not even now anxious about her old friend. The doctor had said she was not ill, only languid and dispirited, and she believed him. No apprehensions disturbed her as she sat composedly down in her aunt's place at the end of the table and smiled at Norton across the big bowl of roses in the centre.

'And what shall we do to amuse ourselves this afternoon?' she asked. 'Shall we forgive Toby's bad behaviour upon another occasion, and go out in the dog-cart? I am sure it is too lovely an afternoon for even you to be busy.'

'I thought of going over to see Lady Mainwaring,' he answered, rather slowly.

'Lady Mainwaring?' repeated Virginia, opening her eyes with some surprise at her own proposition having been received with so little alacrity.

'Yes.' Then, after a pause, with somewhat heightened colour, 'Has it not struck you, Virginia, that Mrs. Stansfield has no intention of returning here on Tuesday; in time for our wedding.'

'It has struck me that her precipitate retreat was intended to annoy me,' answered Virginia, evasively. 'But, if so, I am glad to say that it has missed its aim.

It does not annoy me in the least. At first, it is true, I was hurt by the unkindness of it; but I will not think about that any longer. It is not worth while.'

'But I must think for you,' he answered, in a low voice, looking a good deal disconcerted.

'By all means take up my quarrel, if you please,' cried Virginia, lightly, totally unconscious of his thoughts. 'Only why should we drag poor Lady Mainwaring into the fray?'

'Because there is no one else.' And then, stopping short, 'See, Virginia, go and tell Mademoiselle Joseph what I have said.'

'It will be better for a woman to tell her,' he said to himself. 'I cannot.'

CHAPTER X.

'Yes, my dear child, there is no doubt whatever about it. You shall come to Hinton with me.'

It was Lady Mainwaring who spoke, and she spoke with decision, glancing for approval at Mademoiselle Joseph, who, with a faint flush upon her sallow cheeks, in her turn looked somewhat anxiously at Virginia. But the girl took little notice of either of them. She was seated in the low window-seat beating her little foot impatiently yet softly upon the thick carpet. There was a slight contraction upon her brow, and her eyes were bent upon the floor.

'Come, Virginia, why should not you

N 2

drive back with me this very evening?' pursued the old lady. ' Is it so great a penance to spend a few days at Hinton?'

' On the contrary, it would be very pleasant, only—only that——' She stopped, colouring deeply as, turning her face full upon her old friend, she asked, ' Did Mr. Stansfield ask you to take me away?'

' He did, and he was perfectly right.' Lady Mainwaring never, under any circumstances, shrank from the plain, unvarnished truth. ' Naturally he thought that it would be better for you to be with me. You need not be angry at his consideration for you, Virginia. If your aunt did not return, and you were here alone, your marriage would have been unavoidably, perhaps indefinitely, postponed. That was possibly her intention; but you can be married from Hinton as well as from Stansfield. You need not be angry with Norton.'

' I am not angry,' she answered, in a

low voice; but her quick flush had faded,
leaving her somewhat pale. This then had
been his meaning, and she had been so
absolutely unconscious of it. A pang of
keen mortification shot through her heart,
a sense of undeserved shame at once
angered and depressed her. She understood now the meaning of Mademoiselle
Joseph's hesitating hints. They had all
agreed that it was not fitting she should
remain at Stansfield, everyone had seen it,
everyone had known it but herself. And
Norton! this must have been what he
meant when he said that he must take
thought for her. 'Well,' said Virginia,
angrily to herself, 'he might have spared
himself the trouble.'

When she found that he had gone
out and would not return until the
dinner-hour, she hurried on her preparations for departure so that she might
not see him again, and when he came
over on the morning after her arrival at

Hinton she refused to see him. She was by Mademoiselle Joseph's bedside, for the agitations of the previous day had increased her weakness, and this morning she had found it impossible to rise. She was sleeping after a disturbed night when Lady Mainwaring, opening the door, softly beckoned Virginia out of the room.

'Norton is waiting for you downstairs.'

'I cannot come,' she answered, quickly, 'I cannot leave Mademoiselle Joseph.'

For once Lady Mainwaring's kind voice grew stern.

'That is nonsense, Virginia, and, what is more, it is unkind and unreasonable. You are still angry with him, but you have no right to be angry. Remember, I do not blame you, but he was right. You could not have remained at Stansfield alone with him, for it is very plain that Mademoiselle Joseph could not have been with you.'

But Virginia was too proud to touch

upon the subject which had already broken
up her night's rest with the remembrance
that it was Norton to whom it had been
left to bring home to her the sense of her
defenceless position. A multitude of new
and conflicting ideas were fighting together in a confused medley upon the
battle-field of her mind; new and bewildering lights were breaking in upon
her inward vision. No, even though she
longed to see his dark eyes once more bent
upon her, and to feel the firm clasp of his
hand, she would not see him again—not
yet.

'I cannot see him to-day,' she repeated.

'You will regret it,' cried Lady Mainwaring, with uncontrolled irritation. 'You
are making a mistake. He is not a man
to be played with, and if you will not see
him to-day you will not see him again
until the eve of your wedding. He has
been summoned to London on important
business, and cannot return until Monday.'

'Then I will see him on Monday,' answered Virginia, obstinately. 'I shall have time,' she said to herself, ' to forget what has happened.'

Lady Mainwaring gave her no opportunity to reverse her hasty decision ; she went sweeping away down the corridor in high displeasure to give Mr. Stansfield his answer.

' What did he say ?' she could not help asking when she saw the old lady again.

' He said nothing,' she answered, sharply. ' He is too proud to complain. Besides, he has troubles of his own just now. Troubles of which you, Virginia, know little.'

' No,' thought the girl, bitterly. ' He does not consult me. I am still a child in his eyes, an amusement in his hours of leisure; but I have nothing to do with his cares and sorrows.'

Monday has come, and it is the eve of Virginia's wedding-day. It is already late afternoon; the long, pointed shadows of the lines of cypresses which fringe the western lawn lie black upon the turf. It has been a sultry day; even the flowers are drooping from the heat, and the doors and windows of the house are all set wide open. Virginia has wandered out alone into the garden. A restless desire to escape from Mademoiselle Joseph's anxious eyes, and from Lady Mainwaring's shrewder suspicions, has forced her into solitude. She has had her will. All the ordinary accompaniments of a wedding have been foresworn; a simple white dress hangs in her wardrobe, but she has ordered no other bridal garments; it is not worth while, since she will not as yet put off her mourning, and 'it is not as if I were coming to him penniless,' so she has said. 'I need not be a burden. I am glad, at least, that I am rich.' And they have made her no answer. Not, at this last moment, can they dare to tell her the truth.

She has seated herself under the south wall of the house; a jessamine spreads its dark leaves and pale, starry blossoms against the dull red brick-work above her head; some scattered rose leaves lie in the folds of her black dress, and upon the gravel walk at her feet. Her hands lie idly in her lap, and yet, though unoccupied, she is neither listless nor abstracted; on the contrary, every now and then, at some trivial sound, the colour flushes in her cheeks, and a new light comes into her eyes. Is it possible, she says to herself, that this is what he meant when he asked her if she loved him? These last days have passed very heavily. She longs and yet almost dreads to see him again; and it is very late, and as yet he has not come. Can it be that he is angry; and, if he is, has he not a right? So sitting, with her dark head bent and her eyes upon the ground, she hears quick, firm footsteps

approaching on the other side of the angle
of the wall; and the next instant, with
trembling limbs and a beating heart, she
stands up and irresolutely advances a step
or two to meet him.

Norton too hesitates for an instant, his
eyes eagerly noting each line of her slight,
graceful figure; her blue eyes darkened
by their long lashes; the trembling smile
upon her parted lips; the flush of delicate
colour in her cheeks; and her great fair-
ness strikes with a fresh surprise upon his
heart. Yes, and what is this new look in
her eyes, as her glance falls beneath his,
whilst her hand burns feverishly in his
clasp.

'Virginia, my fair little love, are you
glad to see me again?' he cried, as he took
her in his arms.

For an instant she hid her face upon his
shoulder, and then she pushed him a little
away and laughed softly.

'I was sorry that I did not wish you good-bye; that was why I wished you to come back.'

'Was that the only reason?'

'No; I missed you. I have not been happy. I have not been good. I have vexed Lady Mainwaring and worried poor Mademoiselle Joseph.'

'Now all that is past, and to-morrow it will be past for ever. You know, when people are married, they are good and happy for ever afterwards.'

'That is only in fairy tales,' cried Virginia, shaking her head. 'And I am too old for fairy tales.' Then, with a rapid change of subject: 'Tell me, what have you been doing all this time in London?'

'Trying to put the crooked straight; an unprofitable task.'

'And you will not tell me what you have been about. I understand.' She moved a little away from him, and drew her brows together. 'You think that I need know nothing of your cares or your troubles.'

'My dear child,' he said, kindly, 'why should you desire to be so well versed in this world's disenchantments? Believe me, it is far better to be content not to know. Illusions make up a great part of the happiness of youth.'

'But I do not wish to be deceived,' she persisted. 'If anyone ever deceived me (even, as they supposed, for my own good) wilfully and of set purpose, I would never forgive them. I would never trust them again.'

'Do not make rash vows;' but there was a shade of uneasiness in his voice.

Though he felt sure of her at last, on this the eve of their wedding-day, nevertheless he could not but remember that she had been, as she would have said, 'deceived,' and that she had a woman's pride and an untutored will which had never yet been bent but under the yoke of love. No, she must never know until—until she loved him.

They wandered for a while up and down the garden walks, talking but little and at intervals. He had always been somewhat silent and there was a new, strange shyness upon Virginia this evening from which she had no power, perhaps no desire, to be free.

The sunset lights were burning low in the west, the birds' songs were hushed; a great stillness and peace brooded over the land. He walked by her side filled with an unspeakable gladness of which the harmonious loveliness of nature seemed to be but the fitting accompaniment.

Yet when she said that she must leave him he did not gainsay her. As she opened a French window and stepped into the house, he too walked across the garden and took his way to Stansfield. To-night the silent heavens above him and the old woods and pastures about his home would be his best companions.

In the meantime, Virginia, as she entered the drawing-room, had found herself face to face with Lady Mainwaring. The old lady was standing over Mademoiselle Joseph's helpless figure as she lay back in an arm-chair with an open letter in her hands, sobbing tremulously under her breath.

'It is so cruel,' she cried; 'so heartless and cruel!'

'Who has been cruel?' asked the girl, coming forward with an indignant light in her eyes.

'Oh, I cannot bear to tell you. Your aunt has written to me in such terms. No doubt she has said the same things in her letter to you.'

'Which you should not have seen if only a little common-sense might have been used in the matter,' muttered Lady Mainwaring.

But, in the meantime, Virginia had taken her unopened letter and that addressed to Mademoiselle Joseph from her old friend's trembling fingers, and, calmly lighting a taper at the writing-table, stood reading them by its light.

There was a silence of a few minutes whilst Mademoiselle Joseph checked her sobs and Lady Mainwaring watched the girl, from under her bent brows, with keen interest and some sympathy; but, after those few minutes, Virginia folded up the letters and laid them down, and she looked back at the two regarding her with slightly heightened colour but no other sign of emotion.

'Yes,' she said, 'Aunt Charlotte repeats herself in her letter to me. She says that Norton is marrying me because he cannot help it, because I have been thrust upon him by circumstances, because a report was circulated in the neighbourhood that I was engaged to him, some time ago, and that the facts of the case bore it out. That it is disgraceful that we should be married with such unseemly haste thus in her absence ;' she caught her breath for a moment, and then with a scornful move-ment she thrust the letters aside, and the smile with which she looked round at them was sweet and frank as ever. 'Poor Aunt Charlotte! her arrows, even though they are poisoned, can do us no harm; and yet,' more softly, 'I am sorry.'

'What courage!' cried Mademoiselle Joseph, admiringly. 'I so feared, my be-loved child, that you . . .'

'That I might be angry?' asked Virginia, carelessly. 'Well! I was angry for the moment. But you see I know . . .' for the first time she turned her face aside and walked to the window. She would have said, 'I know that Norton loves me,' but something forbade her to utter her thought aloud even to these two women with whom she was so familiar.

'We will not talk about it any longer,' she said, a little hastily.

'But I must write, I must send her some kind of answer; will anyone tell me what I am to say?' asked Mademoiselle Joseph.

'There is only one thing to be said;' and Virginia smiled. 'It is too late.'

'Because you are going to be married to-morrow?'

'Yes, because I am going to be married to-morrow, and for other reasons which she would not understand.'

She kissed her old friend and would not leave her until her spirits were more composed. She did not any longer shun even Lady Mainwaring's curious glances. She answered her questions without hesitation; her eyes were bright and her cheeks slightly flushed. Lady Mainwaring, as she looked at her, said to herself that she did not wonder at Norton, the girl was in truth wonderfully pretty.

But when at last Virginia could shut herself up in her room, she blew out the lights and kneeling by the window laid her head down upon her folded arms in utter dejection. The night wind ruffled the soft masses of her brown hair but could not avail to cool her fevered cheeks, whilst under cover of the friendly darkness the tears which she had hitherto restrained fell thick and fast.

'I would not let them see that I was hurt,' she said to herself. 'I would not let them see that I was afraid. It is not their fault that I am lonely. And they shall not imagine that he has hurried me, or say that I am not happy. I could be happy if only I were sure . . .' She stopped for a moment and her heart beat fast against the window-sill upon which she was leaning, and even though she was all alone in the dark the colour rushed to her cheeks. 'Why should I ask myself questions; it is a great mistake. If I would

o 2

not answer his it was because I could not
answer my own.'

But long after the rest of the household
were asleep she remained still a silent
and solitary figure, with her head bowed
upon her hands; and the faint starlight
shone through the mists of the hot night,
and the scent of the clematis hung heavily
in the still air, and an oppression as of
death lay upon her heart—and it was the
eve of her marriage day.

'It seems like a judgment,' murmured
Mademoiselle Joseph, as arrayed in wedding
garb of lavender silk and antiquated fashion,
she crossed the hall and opened the door
to take one more despairing look at the
weather. For the sultriness of the night
had been broken by a storm; jagged clouds
spread their black edges against the summer sky, the rain fell in torrents, the
brilliant beauty of the flower-garden was
dimmed, creepers had been torn from the

wall, tall hollyhocks leaned disconsolately away from their supports; and every now and then the light of the morning had paled before the vivid glare of the lightning. Even now at ten o'clock the heavens were still overcast, and the raindrops splashed merrily in the puddles.

Mademoiselle Joseph leaned out her head, and her best cap was sprinkled in a moment. She drew back again, murmuring disconsolately,

'What a misfortune, it is so like a judgment!'

'A judgment! and upon whom, may I inquire?' asked Lady Mainwaring's sharp voice behind her. 'Surely we are none of us conscious of meriting one. I, for my part, never took part in a marriage with less regrets and less remorse. There is generally, almost always, a shadow in the background. But what there is in this case to distress us is more than I can imagine. They love one another as much as can be expected in this matter-of-fact nineteenth century. He is rich and reliable, and will do his best to take care of her; she is pretty and sweet-tempered, and will make him a charming little wife. What more can you desire?'

'But a wedding without a relation, almost without a friend,' cried Mademoiselle Joseph, who could not be at all reconciled to the absence of bridesmaids and wedding-cake, and the want of ceremony about the whole affair. 'Virginia, poor child, she cannot but feel it; she wept last night.'

'Hush!' said her old hostess, quickly cutting short her lamentations, for there was a soft rustle of a silken gown in the corridor above, and the next instant they both turned to see Virginia stepping down the stairs.

If she had wept the night before, she bore no traces of it now. Her eyes were shining, and, though she was somewhat pale, there was a smile upon her lips. Her veil, thrown back from her brow, rested lightly on her hair. In one hand she held some white rosebuds, and with the other she was fastening a spray of orange-blossom in her dress.

'Does not this prove me to be a bride indeed,' she cried smiling. 'See, I have, as you wished it, a white veil and orange blossoms.'

But all the time she was saying to herself, 'They shall never know; no one shall ever know.'

It was as if in a dream that she entered the carriage which was waiting. Lady Mainwaring was saying something, but she did not know what it was. Her bare hands were clasped together tightly upon her lap; they were cold as ice, and her heart seemed to stand still; and yet Lady Mainwaring said to herself she was very glad that she was not going to break down, she had so feared that she would miss her father.

'That is right,' she said, approvingly. 'We shall not have a weeping bride;' and Virginia smiled again, though she did not speak.

In a few minutes they have reached the door of the little church which is at the park gates; only one or two curious women and children are clustered about it; but the rain has ceased, and the sun shines out brightly on the long glistening grass and the ancient tombstones. Still as in a dream, with the curious sense upon her of having gone through the same experience before, Virginia advances up the narrow aisle. Old Mr. Everard is there, and he comes forward, shakes hands, and offers her his arm; she remembers now that she heard he was staying last night at Stansfield. But, even if she had not heard it, she would not to-day be surprised at anything. She only feels for an instant the kind reassuring clasp of Norton's fingers and meets his dark eyes bent upon her with a grave smile; and then the service begins. The old rector is absent from home, and a young shy curate is there in his place. He appears to be nervous, and blunders once or twice in the service; but it is soon over.

They are in the vestry, and the registers have been signed; Mademoiselle Joseph has kissed her with plentiful tears, and even Lady Mainwaring's embrace is somewhat agitated; but Virginia has not shed a tear. For an instant she looks around her as if bewildered, and the little group at the church porch with the swaying green boughs of the old limes above it looks like a picture whose meaning she is vainly endeavouring to discover; but she treads steadily on the flags of the church-yard path which for a moment had seemed to give way beneath her feet; and in another minute she is driving away with Norton beside her, and she turns her flushed face and sparkling eyes upon him.

'I did not cry; no one can say that I cried.'

'I did not exact it,' he answers, gently; and he only clasps more closely the little hand upon which he has put his ring. He thinks that he understood her better when looking up at him she had first said, 'But I do like you; I like you very much.' He has broken, perhaps with rash and precipitate fingers, that old tie of friendly liking and frank fellowship. What has he in its place?

He cannot forbear to question himself; but he is too wise as yet to question Virginia.

CHAPTER XI.

A MONTH has passed; it is the end of
September, and the orthodox honeymoon
is over. Mr. Stansfield and his bride are
expected to return in the evening. How
have these four weeks passed? so Mademoiselle Joseph wonders, yearning over
her child entrusted to this reserved and
unresponsive Englishman; so Lady Mainwaring speculates with a good deal of
curiosity not unmixed with misgiving.
Yes, how is it with them now? so Mrs.
Stansfield too asks herself as she sits await-
ing their arrival in the drawing-room with
an angry contraction on her brow. For
they are not returning, as Mr. Stansfield

had meant that they should return, to an empty house. Business matters have imperatively demanded his presence, but at the last moment Mrs. Stansfield has written to say that her arrangements cannot be so soon completed, and he has had no resource but to leave her and Emmeline in possession of their old rooms. It is disagreeable, but inevitable, for she has some reason upon her side. It is difficult for her to leave her old home upon such short notice.

'It will only be for a little time;' so he said to Virginia. 'And remember, if you have cause of complaint, at whatever inconvenience, a change shall be made.'

Virginia shook her head and laughed.

'I am not afraid.'

'What a favourite formula of yours that is,' he said, smiling. 'At any rate, however hackneyed, it has the merit of truth; but please remember that a retreat may be the best part of valour, and if the worst

came to the worst, we might absent ourselves again for a time.'

'What! and leave Aunt Charlotte in
possession of the field? Indeed I will not.
I liked travelling. It was delightful to
see so many beautiful places; but, now we
are at home, I like my own fireside best,
and I will not go away again.'

Many such speeches had Virginia made
of late, taking a frank, childlike pleasure,
as it were, in her new position. He could
not doubt that she was happy; and a keen
sense of pleasure possessed him when he
remembered that her happiness was in-
separably connected with himself. Never
had anyone been more destitute of other
friends or advisers. Yes, in the end, he
must even by force of circumstances compel
her to love him.

And now they had driven under the
portico. The bell had been rung, and the
door was opened. Once again it was
autumn; a dark, chill evening, like that

upon which she had first seen Stansfield—
a year ago. The butler's solemn countenance was broken by a smile, which he in
vain endeavoured to repress. He had a
strong sense of his own dignity, but he
had known Norton since he was a boy,
and the affection which he and the other
old servants bore to him even outweighed
their dislike of his step-mother.

'You must give Mrs. Norton Stansfield
a welcome, Watkins,' said Norton, and
Virginia held out her hand to the old
man; but, though she did not seem to
miss it, he perceived, with some bitterness,
that it was the only welcome she was
likely to receive.

She stood for an instant, looking round
her with a smile. The glow of the fire on
the wide hearth shone upon the wains-
coated walls and old furniture. Ponto
came to meet them, wagging his tail with
the slow cordiality of old age at the sight
of his master; it looked very warm and

homelike after the cold duskiness outside.

'Are you glad to be at home again?' asked Virginia, looking over her shoulder at her husband.

Glad! He wondered if she would ever know how glad. Though his smile was grave, it was very sweet, as he took her hand and led her on; for Mrs. Stansfield and Emmeline must be in the drawing-room, and the meeting could not longer be delayed.

'By this time he will have found out his mistake,' Mrs. Stansfield had said that after-noon. 'I am only curious to see if he will know how to conceal it. He has a great deal of pride; still there are some wounds that it is impossible to conceal. It will not be long before he discovers that he has married a child, and a child who does not even love him.'

'It must be much better than having a wife who adores you,' observed Emmeline. 'It is very fatiguing to be worshipped, it engenders a certain stiffness of attitude; it is like sitting for your photograph, you feel bound to appear at your best; and for your own wife to be in love with you is an aggravation of the evil. You cannot escape from it, you are allowed no respite.'

'You talk absurdly,' cried Mrs. Stansfield, who had never yet managed to understand her daughter, ' and, even if you were right as to Norton, what about Virginia? Is she not certain sooner or later to fall in love with some one?'

' At any rate, we need not anticipate evils, mamma.'

But all the same Miss Stansfield, like her mother, had her doubts.

' I am not so certain that *she* is not in love with him already,' she said to herself; ' and, if it is so, what will happen when she discovers that he has married her out of pity?'

Emmeline felt really sorry for her cousin, and she had been upon the point of going into the hall to meet her this evening, but she remembered that the door would be open, and that there was an east wind blowing, and she had a cold; so she remained over the fire, whilst her mother busied at her writing-table, affected not to hear the sounds of the arrival.

When the door opened, however, they both involuntarily looked up, and Mrs. Stansfield, as upon that evening a year ago, came forward to meet her niece, but this time she did not lay her hands upon the girl's shoulders, nor did she say, 'Welcome to Stansfield.' This young girl who was to reign as mistress there in her stead was most unwelcome to her, and she was at no pains to conceal it. She kissed her indeed, and said something about the weather and her journey, but all the time, as upon that other occasion, she was taking a mental inventory of her capabilities, only now she was no longer anxious to turn them to the best advantage, but, on the contrary, wondering how she might get the better of them.

And she could not help perceiving that Virginia's charm was even greater than when she had seen her first. It was not in vain that she had wept over the rending of a bond which seemed as if it must have torn her very life in twain; as a flower which, though beaten down by the storm, raises its head in renewed beauty in the morning sunshine, so in like manner her youth had triumphed over sorrow. Her smile was as spontaneous, her look as untroubled, and her words as ready as of old; no coldness of reception, no memory of past unkindness, depressed her. She returned her aunt's greeting courteously, she asked after Emmeline's health as if she had parted from her but yesterday. She looked round the familiar room with the same free and careless glance which she had bestowed upon it on her first arrival. And Mrs. Stansfield, noting

the clear light in her eyes and the health-
ful colour in her cheeks, involuntarily
exclaimed,

'You look well.'

' I am perfectly well,' she answered,
smiling. 'We have had a delightful journey, but now I am very glad to be at
home again.'

Mrs. Stansfield's brow clouded visibly.
She had imagined that at least Virginia
would have felt a little insecure in her
new position, and that she would still be
in absolute command of the house and all
within its walls; and already this young
girl, with exasperating unconsciousness,
had shown symptoms of independence.

' Dinner is at eight,' she observed, after
a moment's pause.

' But we have dined already,' answered
Virginia, who had anticipated this, and
had declared that she would not pass the
first evening beneath her husband's roof
under the constraint of Mrs. Stansfield's

uncongenial presence. She laid aside her hat and cloak, however, and went and sat down in a friendly fashion on the arm of Emmeline's chair.

' So you have survived one month's *têtc-à-tête* with Norton ?' observed Miss Stansfield, looking up at her curiously.

' Why not ?' asked the girl ; but, though she strove to speak lightly, she could not suppress a flush of indignation, and Emmeline, still watching her with cold, observant eyes, said to herself, ' It is very strange, but I believe that I was right ; she must be in love with him.'

' Oh ! I meant nothing personal,' she said aloud. ' Pray do not take the trouble to be offended. I did not ask if Norton had found it tedious ; that might have been an indiscreet question, perhaps.'

' Not if he were here to answer it.'

Virginia still spoke quickly, and looked round for her husband ; but, his short parley with his step-mother being over, he had quitted the room.

'You seem very secure,' said Emmeline, laughing. Then, in a softer tone: 'I wonder, Virginia, what kind of fairy at your birth marked you out for happiness, and ordained that you should find the sunshine beneath every cloud; there must be some magic about it. You do not let us into your secret.'

'I do not understand why any magic should be needed,' she answered. She spoke rather coldly, and gathered up her cloak as she spoke as if to leave the room.

'Now do not be silly, Virginia. I do not grudge you your good spirits; on the contrary, I like people about me to be cheerful. I should have liked Norton better if he was not always so gloomy; and please remember that it is magnanimous of me not to quarrel with you. Certainly I do not pretend to any great affec-

tion for Stansfield, but I am accustomed
to it, and I hate changes. Now, if you
had not married Norton, we might have
remained here.'

' But Norton married me !' said Virginia,
laughing, perhaps to avoid a discussion of
this fact; and she went away, leaving the
mother and daughter alone together.

'What effrontery!' exclaimed Mrs. Stansfield, rising from her writing-table. 'It is
really insufferable. She has no sense
whatever of her proper position. I should
have imagined that in this house at least
some respect was due to me. She might
at any rate remember that I am her aunt.'

' But you do not remember that you did
your best to insult her. And she is not
revengeful; if she were, she would have
shown that letter to Norton, and we should
not be here to-day. I see that she is quite
indifferent to your anger, but, unless she
forced a quarrel, what other attitude was
possible to her ? No, our last move has

been played, and you know I tried to dis-
suade you from it; nothing is left but to
keep the road open for a retreat.'

' I am not so sure of that,' answered her
mother, more in her usual manner. She
was not anxious to take Emmeline into
her counsel, and she said no more; but
she was a determined woman; she would
leave no stone unturned to gain her own
ends; she would not despair until she was
altogether beaten from the field. At this
moment she was still at Stansfield, and she
had at least one ally whose aid she had
not as yet invoked; she had still one formidable charge to bring forward. Virginia
should be taught to know her proper place,
and, when humbled and discouraged, it
might not be so impossible for the former
mistress of the house to retain some
authority at Stansfield.

In the meantime, in happy ignorance of
these machinations, Virginia sat on a low
stool by the library fire, gazing with

thoughtful but yet untroubled eyes into
its glowing caverns. She would not
look up when her husband entered the
room, though the colour deepened in her
cheeks. Once more amongst the old
familiar surroundings, her changed position struck her with shy surprise; she
was a little afraid of Norton this evening,
though she would not let him see it.
There was a momentary pause, then he
came and knelt down beside her and laid
his hand, smiling, upon her head. She
trembled a little and tried, but unsuccess-
fully, to lift her eyes to his. He could not
but observe her heightened colour, her
downcast gaze, the unsteadiness of the
little hand which he had taken in his own.

Has he won her at last? His heart
is beating fast and there is a long silence
whilst the fire throws its light over their
two dark heads, and the rich and sober
colouring of the furniture takes deeper
tints; and outside the wild autumnal wind,

as it dashes against the shutters, serves but to heighten the sense of security and warmth within the curtained room.

' Virginia, I have a question to ask you —at last, to-night.'

His words are arrested. Her hand is laid upon his mouth.

' Do not ask it,' she cries, quickly. ' Do not, Norton ;' and she raises herself for an instant to hide her eyes upon his shoulder.

He does not press her, perhaps he has no need. Some day she will tell him of her own free will, if indeed she has not told him already.

He looks down fondly at the shining waves of her brown hair, he presses his lips to her bent head, and in the happy silence he marvels at his most unmerited good fortune, he wonders that a life once so barren should be so richly blessed.

CHAPTER XII.

The hoar frost still glittered in the sun and the light mist of autumn veiled the distance and softened the brilliant colours of the changing foliage. The early frost had blackened the bed of heliotrope, but the dahlias and geraniums were still bright in the borders, and the virginian creeper about the library windows spread a network of crimson against the old grey stones. The rich and ruddy tints of ripened fruit and falling leaves told as in a silent parable the story of the passing year, in which the two great forces of nature, death and life, were so inextricably intertwined.

Virginia ran lightly down the steps of the terrace into the garden; she had no thought of its hidden meaning, but she was glad of the fresh loveliness and the glittering aspect of the October morning. From the step on which she stood she looked out over the smooth turf and shrubberies, the line of dark yew-hedges; the walled-in kitchen-garden, and on to where the enclosures ended in ground broken by wood and pasture, and with a girlish pride she said to herself, 'All this is his, and so it is mine.'

'Virginia, stay a moment,' cried a voice behind her. It was Emmeline, wrapped in a shawl and shivering in the brisk, fresh air, but with more animation than usual in her voice and manner. 'Wait a moment and come back into the shelter of the house. I have something to say to you.'

'Well! let me hear it,' answered Virginia, looking surprised, but at once turning back to the sunny side of the house.

'Marshall is here,' continued Miss Stansfield, still with unusual eagerness. 'And I am afraid that Norton will summarily dismiss him. It would be a great mistake.'

'I thought he was dismissed long ago.'

'Not exactly. He still retains some sort of office, I hardly know what, about the place. It will be best to let him remain. You had better use your influence with Norton, for, if he is dismissed, Marshall will revenge himself upon you.'

'Upon me;' and she laughed. 'What possible harm can he do to me?'

Once more her eyes wandered carelessly over the prospect before her. How sunny the world was, how peaceful and sheltered this old garden, how secure she felt.

'He can make mischief,' pursued Miss Stansfield, 'but if you can only prevail upon Norton to let him remain he will not say to anyone else what he has already said to me. There is no time to be lost, Virginia. Norton will send for him when he comes in, and he is only at the stables. I should not have come out so early if I had not been anxious about it.'

'Do you mean to say that Marshall sent you to me? I am not surprised at him, but I am surprised that you should be his messenger,' cried Virginia, with a little proud movement of her head. 'And upon what possible pretext should I intercede for a man whom I utterly despise? who steals into people's houses, and reads their letters and will lie in any way to his own advantage.'

'Oh, how young you are to talk of despising anybody,' sighed Emmeline. 'A wasp, remember, is not a formidable antagonist, but it can sting. Look,' suddenly breaking off, 'there is Norton going round by the back entrance; unless you go to him at once it will be too late.'

'I am certainly not going to him. I

have no desire to forestall Mr. Marshall.'

'Then he will go to mamma, and there will be one of those scenes which upset me for a week. How unreasonable you are! And you will be sorry afterwards when it is too late. Well! I have done my best, I can say no more.'

'Do not make yourself unhappy,' said Virginia, gently, looking down at her. 'I have needed your pity before, but I do not need it now;' and she went away, lightly brushing the dew from the grass as she walked across the lawn.

The sky was an azure arch above her head, the low-lying pastures and the autumn woods, the sheep upon the distant hills, and all the familiar aspect of the country as it lay before her was framed in it as in a picture. 'It is a very beautiful world,' said Virginia to herself. And she was in no hurry to return to the house. She had not understood Miss Stansfield's warning, but she knew that her husband would be

occupied with business, and there was no
one else there for whose company she felt
any desire. It was better to be alone and
out of doors. Besides, if Emmeline were
right, and there was to be any domestic
disturbance, she did not wish to be present
at it, it could have nothing to do with
her.

It was not until past mid-day that she
turned back towards the house : even then
she lingered on the doorstep, reluctant to
leave the sunny solitude of the garden.
Marshall was leaving the drawing-room as
she came in, but perceiving her at the
door he turned and quitted the hall by a
side entrance. He must have a bad conscience, the girl thought, rather scornfully
observing his manœuvre, and she was
passing on to the foot of the stairs when
the drawing-room door opened once more,
and her aunt's voice arrested her.

'Will you come to me for a few minutes,
Virginia ?'

She spoke more gently than had been
her habit of late, and Virginia had no just
reason to refuse her request, though she
was anxious to escape as soon as possible,
and would not sit down but remained
standing at a little distance from the
sofa upon which Mrs. Stansfield was seated, drawing the ribbons of her hat, which
she had taken off, idly through her
fingers.

'This is a very serious matter, Virginia,'
began her aunt. 'It is true, I had warned
you. I knew that you were very young,
very indiscreet, but I did not expect that
anyone, not even a servant with a spite
against you, could have brought such a
charge. What could now be done?' she
asked, with real or affected consternation.
'What can be done to silence unkind
tongues and atone for the indiscretions of
the past?'

'But what is it? What am I accused
of?' she started as if awakening from a

dream. She was not afraid, she was not
even sorry, but she did not understand.
'What can Marshall have said? Yet no,'
with a sudden, involuntary movement of
disdain. 'I do not wish to hear what he
has said.'

'You shall at least have an opportunity
to deny it,' answered Mrs. Stansfield, in a
tone which implied the opportunity would
be given in vain. 'As I have said, I knew
that you were too little upon your guard,
but I did not know that you were in the
habit of seeking Norton in his private rooms
at all hours. Yet what am I to believe
when Marshall tells me he saw you alone
together at twelve o'clock at night in the
library! I will touch upon no other
point. Answer me only as to this. Is it
true or false?'

And then, to her aunt's and Emmeline's
profound amazement, the indignant colour
died out of the girl's cheeks, her eyes
looked down at them no longer proud and

startled, though still a little contemptuous —and she broke into a laugh.

'And did Mr. Marshall tell you what he was doing on that occasion?' she cried. 'Did he tell you that I came down because I saw him from my bed-room window stealing out of the house, where he had [been pillaging Norton's papers? Did he tell you that he fled before me on the wings of his bad conscience, even before Norton came in, even before Jack could vanquish him, as he was longing to do, with the garden-syringe?'

'And was that all you thought of?' Mrs. Stansfield's astonishment was for once perfectly genuine, and she had not recovered from it. 'Did you never think what a construction might be put upon your conduct? Besides, that is not the only time . . .'

'When I thwarted Mr. Marshall's schemes. No, I am quite aware of that, Aunt Charlotte, and I, upon my part, had no accomplice but Jack, and by no fault of his own he had not an active part to play.'

Mrs. Stansfield was silent for a moment. She was utterly at a loss. She had expected anger and tears; a storm, in which she alone retaining her self-possession should have obtained an easy mastery. She was absolutely baffled by Virginia's frank and disdainful unconcern. Was it insensibility, was it bravado? she could not tell. She only knew that it made it impossible for her to work upon her fears, and she was perforce obliged to adopt another tone. Emmeline, from her sofa, watched with quiet amusement the altered position of the two combatants; the judge so crestfallen and perplexed, the culprit so unconscious of her offence.

'It was a lamentable indiscretion,' said Mrs. Stansfield, after a silence, as if speaking to herself. She needed time to form a new plan of attack, and she did not know what else to say. 'Still,' suddenly looking up as if enlightened, 'I can believe that you are only very young and very foolish. The question now is how to repair your error. You see,' speaking slowly, 'the facts are against you. These reports having arisen with or without cause, you next, in my absence, rush into this hasty marriage. Under the circumstances, it is possible Norton acted for the best. Nevertheless, not a single relative is present at it, and it takes place from the house of a comparative stranger. Still I am ready to condone the past, and as long as I remain here,' with emphasis, 'as long as I am in the house, if you will be guided by me, I will stand by you.'

Virginia, too, paused a moment before making any answer. Perhaps this sudden change of tactics bewildered her. She stood still, looking down at the shifting sunshine which, streaming in at the window, lay upon the rich colours of the carpet at her feet. Then she suddenly lifted her head, and looked round with a smile.

'Stand by me! But my husband will do that,' said Virginia; and then she went away, quickly shutting the door behind her.

'Oh, mamma, you have done your best, but it is no use : you are no match for Virginia,' observed Emmeline. 'I told you it would be no use. You will only have made us all uncomfortable together.'

'Uncomfortable!' echoed Mrs. Stansfield, scornfully. 'I really believe that if you can have an easy sofa, and no draughts, and no exertion is required of you, you desire nothing more from life.'

'Then since my wants are so simple they should be supplied,' answered her daughter. 'After all, other people are much more exacting. But you are not quite right, mamma; I have also some value for domestic peace and a quiet mind, and that is why I wanted you to let Virginia alone. It will not suit me to move in a hurry, and, if Virginia tells Norton the accusations you have brought against her, it strikes me that our stay here will be of the shortest. She does not fear the consequences of what you call her past indiscretions, indeed she is evidently unaware that she has committed any; she has no wish to shelter herself under your irreproachable character; as to her reception in the neighbourhood, she has not given it a thought, and she is altogether indifferent to other people's opinion. So you see that all the arguments which you intended to bring to bear are powerless.'

'And I do not need you to assure me of it,' answered Mrs. Stansfield.

She was baffled, and she knew it. She had come, as most of us come sooner or later, to a bad turning-point in life, an she had no resource but to take the rough and distasteful path marked out for her.

On all sides she saw nothing but disappointment—her stepson secure of his rights and his inheritance, herself driven from her old position of authority and power which, though it might be of small consequence in other people's eyes, was of overweening value in her own; she would be deprived of all those countless duties which fall to the share of the mistress of a county house, she would be reduced to living in a smaller house with fewer servants, and have little to occupy her but her scanty correspondence and Emmeline's ailments. Jack's holidays could hardly be looked upon in the light of agreeable interruptions; no, he was her youngest born, but she could never love Jack until he had learnt to rub his muddy boots, and set straight his rumpled collars, and abjure slang and pea-shooters.

And Hartley! With some regretful tenderness she thought of her handsome boy, the only one of her family in whom she felt any natural maternal pride, and he too was, as she chose to believe, banished from his home, and deprived of his rights, by this girl who, with careless unconcern, had thwarted each of her cherished plans. Perhaps even now the thought of Hartley was the sorest one of all. She had some vague misgivings respecting him; she was in truth never easy when he was long absent from her, and at this moment she did not know where he was. He had written to her last from Munich, and he was then on his way home. It was quite possible that he was now in London, but keeping out of her way for reasons of his own. She half-suspected that Norton knew something about him, but was too proud to question her stepson. So, tormented with vague suspicions and embittered by her wrongs, jealous and irritated, she was ready to attack Virginia, the innocent cause of all these ills; and it was exasperating to find that her arrows fell wide of her mark and the bow in her hand was broken.

CHAPTER XIII.

But though Virginia had faced Mrs.
Stansfield's accusations with a careless
pride, which was too unconscious to be
defiant, she had nevertheless left her in
disturbed spirits. Could it be that Norton
had known all this? Had he married her
to defend her? and her cheeks burnt at the
thought. But no, why should she doubt
him? Had he ever deceived her; had he
ever kept anything from her? 'Never, and
I know that he loves me,' she said to herself. 'I am sure of it,' and yet the very
earnestness of the self-assurance betrayed
the little misgiving which stealthily like an
unwelcome uninvited guest had crept into
her mind; alas, it was born not so much of

Mrs. Stansfield's words as of the love whose joys can be only reached through pain. That love new and bewildering was stirring in the girl's heart; she did not as yet acknowledge it to herself; but her cousin was right: she loved him.

Therefore it was that she kept silence. She dared not question him. Too generous to tell of the accusations which had been brought, and yet too frank to affect a confidence which she did not feel, during the days that followed she shrank from his notice, she avoided the library, and took long walks alone in the autumn woods; or paced the walled-in garden when the dusk fell, and the shutters were shut, and there were lights within the house.

'At last mamma has wounded her, poor Virginia,' said Emmeline to herself; but as for Norton he said nothing, he only watched and waited. Was this love in its first shy dawnings, or was it a silent revolt against her new bonds, an unconquerable longing for freedom, none the less strong because unexpressed? He could not tell, but sitting unoccupied and solitary in the library, with bent brows and downcast eyes, he pondered the question. And to one thing at least he made up his mind: he must be alone with Virginia. There should be no further delay; Mrs. Stansfield and Emmeline must leave his house. He got up, shook the hair from his forehead, and, bracing himself for a disagreeable task, went to communicate his decision to his step-mother.

Virginia coming in an hour later bearing a big unwieldy parcel, and looking flushed and elated, found her aunt alone, still sitting in the same position in which Norton had left her. She was thinking that it was of no avail; her fate was sealed, and at least she was glad that she had answered her step-son with dignity and self-control; nevertheless, a deep indignation, a sullen fire of jealousy and resent-

ment, smouldered within her, and at
Virginia's first words it burst into a
flame.

'Where is Emmeline?' cried the girl,
eagerly, as she knelt down upon the floor
and unfolded her parcel. 'She must come
at once, and see what I have for her. Will
she not be pleased? Will not this keep her
warm?' and she passed her fingers up and
down the fur rug, which she had spread
upon the carpet. 'See, Aunt Charlotte.
I have got it down in time for the cold
weather.'

'You!' cried Mrs. Stansfield, with sudden
unreasonable fury. 'You mean that it is
your gift?'

'It is,' answered Virginia, calmly; and
then, with a movement of natural petu-
lance: 'It is none the worse for that.'

'And how can you give who have nothing? Yes, no doubt it is easy to forget
the past; to forget that you came here
friendless and alone to take the place of

others.   Easy to be contented, and glad to
be deceived.'

'I do not know what you mean?' cried
Virginia, colouring, and rising to her feet.
'I am indeed content, I have good reason.
But why should you say that I am de-
ceived.   No one would desire to deceive
me.'

'Not Norton?' asked Mrs. Stansfield,
grimly.   Her irritation must find a vent,
and she had lost all self-control.   'Has no
one, not even your husband, dared as yet
to tell you the truth?   You think that he
married you for love.'

'He did,' cried Virginia.   She was very
pale now, and pressed her hands to her
heart;   but, at whatever cost, his love
should be vindicated.   Since he was not
here to speak for himself, she would speak
for him;   and so, whilst the burning tears
rose to her eyes, and her hands turned
cold as ice, she stood facing Mrs. Stansfield's anger, and cried, 'He did.'

'It was a love very speedily born of compassion,' answered her aunt, her passion cooling under the influence of the girl's intense feeling. 'Was it not when he found out from Mr. Everard that nothing could be saved from the wreck of your fortunes—was it not when he discovered that you were penniless that he asked you to marry him?'

'No, it is not true!' cried Virginia; and yet she knew that she was wounded.

The thrust had gone home; the words, though spoken in ill-will and anger, had a terrible ring of truth. None the less would she strike a last blow in her own defence; for was she not fighting for Norton as well as for herself?

'Ask him!' replied Mrs. Stansfield, laconically. 'If you will not believe me, ask him.'

'But what do you mean? Tell me, Aunt Charlotte. It is not possible. I know . . . I know that I was rich; I

was always told so. Mademoiselle Joseph
spoke of my fortune.'

She stopped, for she could not bring
herself to utter a yet dearer name.

'Fortunes are easily lost, Virginia. It
would seem that you were not so unfortunate, since you only lost one to find
another.'

But Virginia was dumb. She had sunk
down, as if bewildered, on a chair. Her
aunt's sarcasm passed unheeded. 'Can it
be true?' she was saying to herself. 'Can
it be true?'

'Ask Norton,' repeated Mrs. Stansfield.

She rose up and cast one glance over
the girl's dejected figure; then she gathered
her various possessions, her account-books,
her workcase, and silks, together, and with
deliberate footsteps left the room. For
once in her life she had gained a victory
over Virginia.

'Ask Norton.' But, no, she could not do
that. What, ask a question to which she

would not dare to receive the answer?
Pride and love, and every fibre of her
highly-strung nature, rebelled against it.
'No, whatever happens,' she said to herself, 'I cannot ask him; and,' sadly,
'there is no need. Do not acts and looks
speak louder than words? I must be dull
indeed, if I cannot interpret their language.
And, since he has once deceived me, of
what possible value would be his pro-
testations?'

She rose from her seat, passed her hand
for a moment across her heavy eyes, and,
with lagging footsteps, began to mount the
stairs, when a voice behind arrested her.

It was Norton, who was coming towards her with a telegram in his hand.
He looked unusually perturbed, as he
asked her to come into the library. She
turned at once, assenting indifferently. If
it were indeed true; if he had already
deceived her, what could anything else
matter?

'I have had a summons to London, which I cannot well refuse,' he said, abruptly, as soon as the door was closed. 'It is nothing agreeable. You remember just before we married I was obliged to leave you.'

'Yes. I thought that you went to arrange my money affairs and see Mr. Everard,' said Virginia, slowly. She raised her eyes to him with a look he did not understand. 'Now I shall see if Aunt Charlotte was right,' she said to herself. 'If he is true, he will now at least acknowledge that I had no money affairs to arrange. If he does not speak now, I will never trust him again.'

'It was partly on your account,' he answered, 'but chiefly upon Hartley's. He has been in London some time, though his mother does not know it. I always knew that sooner or later he must come to grief. It is no use to enter into particulars, but since he has applied to me I cannot well refuse to go; but,' stretching out his hands for hers, 'I do not like to leave you.'

'Oh, do not let me keep you;' and she drew her hand gently yet decidedly out of his. 'I—I shall do very well.'

He did not answer for a moment. Again with unwelcome persistency the question forced itself upon him : Is this cold rejoinder but the first outward expression of the rebellion against her fate which, during these few weeks, had been silently gathering strength within her.

'Will it be well?' he asked, with rather a sad smile. 'Alone with Mrs. Stansfield and Emmeline? I cannot tell how long I may be away, I might be detained.' And he gave her a quick, keen look, but she had turned her head aside. Perhaps, after all, she thought, bitterly, he was not sorry to be free. He had said nothing of himself, he thought only of her. She would not ask him to remain, still less would she cry, ' Take me with you.'

' And when are you going ?'

' This afternoon. I have no time to lose. I have barely time to catch the three o'clock train.'

He had not meant to speak so shortly, but, stung by her indifference, he would if possible put her to the proof. Surely she could not let him go in this way without a word.

' So soon !' and she involuntarily caught her breath.

' Yes, it is very soon,' answered Norton, and he sat down by the table, and leaning his arms upon it, looked up at her with his dark gloomy eyes. 'It is very soon. The delusion might have lasted a little longer. We have been married barely six weeks, and it is very soon to find that I cannot make you happy, soon to discover that my going or coming is equally indifferent, soon to perceive that to you our marriage is a bondage; yes, I have seen it already in your altered looks, in your daily actions, but never as yet so clearly as to-day. Well, Virginia, I can make you no amends; but at least I have not willingly wronged you. I did it for the best.'

Virginia stood silent. Amazement and anger had for the moment drowned all other feelings. Never before had she seen him so moved; never but once before in the moonlit garden, when he told her of his love, had his habitual self-control deserted him. But the strong tide had overleaped its barriers and flowed all the more swiftly for its past repression. So it was true, he had married her for the best, for her sake, not his own. In her present state of highly-wrought feeling the very admission seemed to be an insult.

'I know,' she answered, in a low voice. 'You did it for the best.'

'And some mistakes are in their nature irrevocable,' he continued, with increased bitterness. 'But there may be alleviations. At any rate I am going away to-day.'

'Do not go in anger,' she faltered. The room seemed to grow dim. Now that this last moment had come, a fear sudden and unreasonable had laid its heavy hand upon her heart. What if he should not come back! What if indeed this cold and hurried parting should be the last!

'Do not be afraid. I cannot, if I would, forget that the error was mine, and mine alone. You did not deceive me, you never said you loved me. I have forgotten, I have been unreasonable for this once, Virginia; but you need not be afraid that I shall commit the same fault again.'

He paused, but she made no rejoinder. Would not even his bitterest reproaches

be less insufferable than the coldness of
estranged affection and disappointed love?
for in one sense she could not doubt that
he loved her as he might have loved a
sister or a child. What were they to do
in the long years before them, without
trust upon her side and wounded affection
upon his?

'We will not say good-bye,' he cried,
and his voice was a little unsteady. 'You
told me once before that you hated the
word, and you were right.'

He dared not look at her again, lest his
resolution should fail him; and the minutes
were passing quickly, it was late already,
and at any moment they might be interrupted. For an instant he took her in his
arms and felt her tremble in his clasp,
whilst he kissed her; and then, with hasty
footsteps, and without a backward look,
he was gone.

Virginia sank down on a chair and
bowed her head in her hands.

'And I, who feared lest I should not love him,' she cried to herself, 'alas! I love him too well.'

CHAPTER XIV.

It was growing dusk, and Emmeline sat alone in the big drawing-room, but she had forgotten to ring for lights, and, though it was chilly, the fire was dying out, and she had paid no heed to it. For once in her life she was oblivious of physical discomforts.

'Why will people be so unreasonable?' she was thinking. 'It is all their own fault. Why should Norton have spoken to mamma before he left? It was not like him. It showed a want of self-restraint; he might have known that, when he said she must leave Stansfield, she would make haste to visit it upon Virginia. And, now the girl is married, what is the use of telling her why he married her? If she liked to imagine that he fell in love with her, the delusion would have done no one any harm. Though she was too proud to say anything, I believe she has taken mamma's assertions terribly to heart. I declare it makes me feel quite wretched. I hate to see Virginia unhappy, she was not meant for it, and, though she is so light-hearted, she is just the sort of girl to throw herself into the river if anything went wrong with her. She is desperately in love with Norton. Oh, what a mistake it all is! Why will people be so foolish?'

Miss Stansfield shook herself with a shiver; she got up and walked irresolutely to the window, and then back to the hearth, and stood over the blackened embers trembling for a moment or two. Finally she moved to the door. It was a great mistake to be soft-hearted, and she was surprised at herself, still she could not leave Virginia to brood over her wrongs alone; some one must speak to her, and so she would make an heroic effort, and would face the draughty passages and mount the stairs to find her.

But Virginia was not in her little sitting-room. The lamp was lighted there, and all things in order, but the room was empty, and the door communicating with her bed-room was locked. In answer to her cousin's knock, however, she answered in her ordinary voice that she would come to her immediately, and in a few minutes she entered. The light fell full upon her face, and Emmeline noticed that there were no traces of tears upon it, and she met her cousin's eyes without embarrass-ment as, coming forward, she knelt down upon the hearth-rug and stirred the fire into a blaze. Yet Emmeline, observing her closely, saw that, as she stretched out her hands to it, a slight shiver passed through her frame.

'How silly you are to shut yourself up

in your bed-room,' she began, in a tone of querulousness which was for the moment partly assumed. 'I daresay you have no fire, and it is no use making yourself ill because you are angry with mamma. I saw you were vexed, that was why I came to find you. I hope you are not going to be so foolish as to make yourself unhappy.'

'Why should I be unhappy?' asked Virginia forcing a smile. 'Have I ever made myself unhappy before at anything which Aunt Charlotte has said to me? It . . it is not the first time.'

'No, but it is the first time that she has touched you. Do not deny it, Virginia.'

'I am not going to deny it,' answered the girl, calmly. 'I had always said that I was glad to be rich. I made no secret of it. I was sorry to hear that I had no money. Very sorry.'

'And yet it need not matter to you now. No, it is not that which troubles you, it is

what she asserted about Norton.   I know;
but why, Virginia . . .'

'Why should I believe her?' the girl
interrupted quickly.   'Yes, why indeed.'

And yet, though her trembling limbs and
beating heart belied her words, she would
have given worlds that Emmeline might
echo them.   Emmeline knew the world,
she had not been blinded, she had looked
on with the calm and unbiassed judgment of a bystander.   Moreover, she was
sorry for her and anxious to console ; surely
she, if anyone, might give her the assurance that Mrs. Stansfield had perverted the
truth, that her words were but the un-
supported testimony of an angry woman,
and that though all the facts might be
against her and her loss of fortune a reality,
it had not been as her aunt had asserted
the motive of her husband's action ; surely
Emmeline at least might upbraid her with
faint-heartedness and tell her still to believe in the love for which she stretched

out her hands with such blind and hopeless yearning, now that she felt it slipping
from her grasp? She dared not turn her
head, but straining her hands together as
she cried, ' Why should I believe her?' she
listened for the answer. But Emmeline,
though anxious to avoid the disagreeable
consequences of sincerity was not un-
truthful.

' You are very unreasonable to disturb
yourself about anything that she may have
said,' she answered, evasively. ' Would
you rather that Norton had married you
because you were an heiress? Why, that
is a thing which happens every day and
nobody thinks any the worse of a man,
on that account.'

' No, I suppose not.'

' Certainly not. Marriages are nearly
always fair or unfair bargains. So much
love weighed against so many temporal
advantages, and the temporalities as a rule
kick the beam. In your case you surely

need have no misgivings. I always told
you that you were far too good for Norton.
If he has given you a home, you have given
him other things which even in my eyes,
Virginia, are more worth having, and to do
him justice he thinks so too. Be satisfied
that he has no regrets; you cannot expect
a man of his age and temperament to be
in love. After a time you would find it
terribly inconvenient if he were.'

'Yes, I understand.'

But, in truth, she understood only that
her last hope had been taken from her,
and the ground was failing beneath her
feet. A multitude of corroborating remembrances crowded unbidden into her
mind. With a rush of shame and confusion, she remembered the money which
he had brought her from London; she remembered how she had said to him, 'I am
glad that I am rich;' how she had never
scrupled to spend freely since her marriage
on any object which pleased her, and what

pleasure he had taken in procuring her
little surprises; how gladly at her desire
he had brought home a magnificent shawl
from Paris for Mademoiselle Joseph. She
who had always hated to be dependent
was indebted for everything she possessed
to a man who did not love her, who had
married her out of a generous pity, awak-
ened by the hard circumstances of her
fate. So she thought with ever-increasing
bitterness, and a desire arose, if possible,
to escape from the miserable complications
of her present position. Miss Stansfield
had judged her rightly when she had said
that any rash act would be possible to the
girl in the first awakening to the knowledge that the bonds which held her were
not the bonds of love.

'It will be better for you both when
we have left,' continued Miss Stansfield.
'These amalgamated households never
answer. I owe you no grudge for turning
us out; though Norton has been rather

hasty, we must have gone sooner or later.'

'Are you going upon my account?'

'Naturally; do you think that Norton would forgive mamma's behaviour to you? I do not blame him for taking your part. He was right, only he need not have been so peremptory. But no doubt it is best. Hartley, for instance, could not well have come here.'

'Yes, yes, I see.'

She felt as if she could bear no more. Everything was against her; she was a burden, an obstacle in everyone's way. Oh! if she could only forget these last feverish months of her existence, and be once more the light-hearted little girl who had spent the summer days beneath the sweet-scented lime-trees at La Vallière, and found them all too short!

'I think Mrs. Stansfield is wishing to see you, Miss Emmeline,' said Mademoiselle Joseph, entering at that moment.

Her figure looked unusually feeble and

her voice was weak. As soon as Miss
Stansfield was gone, she sank down upon
the sofa in an attitude of despondency;
and, preoccupied as she was, Virginia
observed it with quick affection.

'What is the matter?—something is
troubling you.'

'Oh! your aunt! It is wicked of me,
perhaps, to say it, but she is indeed a
terrible woman!' cried the poor governess.
'I have surely always shown her due
deference and respect. But what things
she has made me suffer—what harshness
—what injustice!' and she began to weep.

'Injustice which neither you nor I will
suffer any longer!' cried Virginia, who, for
her part, was far too highly wrought for
tears. 'I have a plan, Mademoiselle Joseph.
There is no place for us in this cold, in-
hospitable country; there is no room for
us in this house. It has all been a terrible
mistake, and you ought to have told me.
You knew that I was penniless; if I had

known it also, I would not have been married. But it is not too late to make some reparation for the past. We have at least enough money to take us back to our old home at La Vallière, where we spent so many happy years. One lives upon so little in France, and the house is still mine; old André and his wife are taking charge of it. Will they not be delighted to see us again ?'

She spoke rapidly; the feverish colour burned in her cheeks and parted lips as she knelt down by her old friend and laid her her hands upon her knees.

'But why? why are we to go?' asked Mademoiselle Joseph, faltering and perplexed.

'Why, because life here is intolerable,' cried Virginia. 'It cannot be endured. It is for no one's happiness that we should remain.'

And yet only that morning how happy she had been. What joy it had been

s 2

to know that his home was hers! The tears which she would not allow to fall darkened her eyes, and she turned her head quickly aside.

'But your husband, my poor child,' objected Mademoiselle Joseph, feebly. 'Do you not see that this is a terrible step which you are contemplating. How can you leave his house, his home, without his consent; and you know well that he would not accord it.'

'No, he would not send me away,' she answered, in a low voice, smiling bitterly. 'That is all the more reason why I should relieve him of my presence which is an embarrassment. There is no time to be lost, a delay would not alter my determination. No! we will not stay here or be made miserable any longer. It is not necessary.'

She spoke firmly, in a tone to which, from her earliest childhood, Mademoiselle Joseph had been accustomed to defer.

She had often disagreed with Virginia but she had never been able to resist her will. She felt at this moment absolutely powerless; if she chose to take this unprecedented step and leave her husband's house that very night, Mademoiselle Joseph would have no power to say her nay.

'Shall you not be glad to see our little peaceful home again,' continued Virginia, persuasively, 'and Mère Lagrange, who used to scold me and kiss me at the same moment, and the good old curé, and the little church, and old Jean smoking his pipe on the bench before the café? Shall you not be glad to be once more in peace and alone with me?'

'Alas! I hardly know how to be glad,' ejaculated Mademoiselle Joseph. 'But when do you propose to go? Not surely without communicating with Mr. Stansfield. Not to-night?'

'No, not to-night, when you are already fatigued and agitated. No, not to-night, but to-morrow morning, when you will have had a good night's rest,' answered Virginia, cheerfully. 'You must not disturb yourself, for I have arranged everything. I shall have a coadjutor in Mary the housemaid, and, as she is under notice to leave, I shall be doing her no injury. The carriage is ordered, the boxes will be packed, and we shall leave at eight tomorrow and catch the boat for Calais. I know you do not like the sea, so we will pass through London. It is perfectly easy.'

' But what will Mr. Stansfield say ?'

Virginia stood up with a little impatient movement and walked away to the window to hide the colour which had rushed to her cheeks; the trembling which passed through her limbs.

'I . . . I do not know; but that need not trouble you ; it is my doing and mine alone, and in the end you will see that it was for the best.'

'Yes, it is best,' she said to herself. 'Best to break this hollow truce between love and enforced fidelity; best that no bitter words should pass between us, no useless explanations; best that we should part whilst we still can say that we were happy before this short month, when I thought that he loved me, is eclipsed by weeks of growing estrangement and unavailing regrets. And at least he will not know how I loved him, no one will ever know;' and she went back to bend again over Mademoiselle Joseph's chair. She assured her once more that all would be well; she painted in vivid colours the peaceful joys of La Vallière, and the tranquil life which awaited them, until the old lady resigned herself to the contemplation of the future, forgetting the precipitate step by which it was to be attained; wearied out, perplexed, but more or less consoled, she at length went to rest, whilst Virginia locked herself into her room and threw herself dressed as she was upon her bed.

Not for one single moment did she swerve from her purpose, and yet even when all alone in the stillness of the night it was in vain to attempt to review the past, in vain to endeavour to reason out the arguments which had so forcibly appealed to her imagination; she could not think, not at least to-night, whilst her brain was fevered and her mind in confusion. She pressed her burning brow against the pillows, and a surging sound of the sea was in her ears, but it was only the October wind in the trees outside. It was in vain to seek for sleep as yet, and she rose once more, and noiselessly with deft fingers went about her preparations. It was not till the morning hours had begun that they were completed. Some parcels she left upon her table, and upon these in legible characters she had written her husband's name; for the rest her boxes and portmanteaux were already locked. And

then at last, with a sigh of relief, she un-
dressed and laid herself down for some few
hours of troubled, half-waking sleep. When
the morning dawned, she would with revived courage set out from the country in
which she had suffered so many disenchantments, and bid farewell to the old house
which had sheltered her during the past
year, and which she had for one short
month called her home.   Once more, with
no companion but her old and faithful
guardian, she would set out to seek her
fortune in a wide and empty world; but,
alas! she had no longer the glad hopes
which had once accompanied her upon her
path; she was shutting the gates of her
earthly paradise behind her, and who could
tell whether they would open again at her
bidding.

CHAPTER XV.

It was still morning when Virginia and
Mademoiselle Joseph stepped out from the
train on to the platform of the London
terminus. Early, very early, before blinds
were yet drawn up or the household fully
awake, before the sun had dispersed the
chilly dimness of the October dawn, they
had quitted Stansfield. Mademoiselle
Joseph, quivering into tears, distressed
and remorseful, had only advanced at that
last moment, because she felt as if her retreat were already cut off. Was not Mary
the housemaid in the secret, and would
she be likely to keep their counsel long?
Was not the carriage already waiting and
the boxes packed? Yes, all these things

were against her, and, when once her treachery should be discovered, how could she ever face Mrs. Stansfield's uncontrolled anger, or, still worse, Norton's stern displeasure? It was terrible to feel herself a traitor, but it would be still worse to be arrested as such. So with trembling, noiseless footsteps she had passed the closed door of Mrs. Stansfield's bed-room and down the shallow-stepped stairs to the hall, where Virginia was already waiting.

And what of Virginia? She stood upon the threshold looking out into the mist. Perhaps it was the chillness of the air which had driven all the colour from her cheeks, but there was no sign of flinching upon her face; her mouth was closely shut, there was a light in her eyes, and her voice was clear and steady. No one could have told of the vain regrets which beset her; of the shadow which fell upon her life when she gazed drearily round the familiar hall, and out across the approach to where the young plantations showed dimly through the clouded atmosphere. By that hall fire-place she had stood when Norton's dark eyes were bent upon her and his kind voice sounded in her ears, telling her to take courage and asking if he was not her friend. Through those shrubberies she had walked in pleasant, familiar converse, with her hand in his, only a few days ago, and now it was all past, like a dream which may not be re-called. Yet was it possible that all was over, and this was her last good-bye to Stansfield? Yes, rather than remain an unwelcome sojourner within his gates she would, in her pride and self-will, close them behind her.

'Oh, can it be right? Is not this a terrible step that we are taking?' sighed poor Mademoiselle Joseph. 'Are you sure that it is right, Virginia?'

'Quite sure,' the girl had answered, with a cold smile.

Nevertheless, when they arrived, alone and uncared for, in the smoke-laden atmosphere and selfish bustle of the great London station, she did not find it so easy to maintain a show of cheerfulness. It was a damp, raw day, and they had an hour or two to wait before proceeding on their journey. It was so early in the year that it had not been thought necessary to light a fire in the waiting-room, and poor Mademoiselle Joseph sat shivering in a depressed attitude over the empty grate. Virginia heaped shawls about her and brought a cup of hot coffee from the refreshment-room, but it was not an inspiriting beverage, and even her assurance that she would soon be drinking coffee on her own native soil failed to win a smile.

'If only I were sure that we were right,' she murmured to herself.

It seemed a very long hour to Virginia as she walked restlessly up and down the platform or came back and forced herself

to speak some word of encouragement to
her old companion. Surely it must be
already two o'clock? but no, she glances
at the clock and sees that there is still
another half-hour of this dreary waiting.
Once more she walks to the door and is
standing, looking out aimlessly at the
throng of passengers, when her own name
falls upon her ears and she involuntarily
starts back with an amazement curiously
compounded of fear and relief.

'Virginia! Can it be you! Good
heavens! what are you doing here?' cries
a cracked boy's voice, and the next instant
Jack has pushed his way through the
crowd and is standing at her side.

'Yes, I suppose I am here;' she smiled,
but her voice was a little tremulous. 'I
did not expect to see you, Jack.'

'And you do not look as if it were
altogether a pleasant surprise,' he answered,
eyeing her more closely. 'I do hope, Virginia, that you have no reason to shun my

unexpected appearance.   Have I not often
told you that perfect openness secures you
against suspicion, and . . .'

'Don't begin to moralize,' interrupted
Virginia, impatiently.   'And I am sure
you are in a hurry.   Do not let me keep
you.'

'Why, how short your temper is!' cried
Jack.   'Have some toffee,' pulling a parcel
out of his pocket, 'then perhaps you will
feel better.   It is first-rate.'

But Virginia declined the proffered
delicacy rather curtly, and made a step
back towards the waiting-room.   Her first
feeling had been one of welcome to Jack,
with his familiar greeting, his dusty jacket,
and his friendly if somewhat painful grasp
upon her hand; but now she began to
dread his small, inquisitive eyes and his
further questions.

'No, stop a minute,' he cried at once,
perceiving her purpose, and laying a detaining hand upon her dress; 'you have

not answered my questions yet, Virginia. Have you remembered that I have now all the rights of a double relationship? have you reflected that I am not only your cousin but your half-brother-in-law? What were you thinking of not to invite me to the wedding? though I understand it was a very shabby affair, with no breakfast or bride-cake. Still I ought to have been asked. And so you are really Mrs. Norton Stansfield. It is quite absurd at your age; and now it is too late to think better of it. But what are you doing here, and where is Norton?'

'I don't exactly know; somewhere in London, I believe,' answered Virginia, with as much unconcern as she could muster.

'I don't exactly know, somewhere in London,' slowly repeating her words. 'Good gracious, Virginia! has he run away from you already?'

'He was summoned to London on business. I do not remember his exact address, but no doubt you could get it at his club. And now I think, if you have nothing else to say, I must go back to Mademoiselle Joseph in the waiting-room.'

She drew up her slight figure, and spoke with an assumption of dignity, but in truth her heart fainted within her. This casual meeting might bring about so many complications, for she could not pledge Jack to secrecy without giving him more of her confidence than she desired, and she began to perceive that his curiosity would not be easily evaded.

'Then, what are you doing here?' cried Jack. 'My word, Virginia, is it possible that *you* are running away from *him?*'

'Certainly not,' she answered, angrily, revolting instinctively against this bald and vulgar suggestion. 'But—but I am going away from Stansfield for a time. I think it is best. I am going back to my old home in France.'

'Oh! what a pity that you have brought

Mademoiselle Joseph with you,' ejaculated her cousin. ' If it had not been for that, I declare I would have bought a frock-coat, and taken my passage with you. You see, I am up here for my *exeat;* but, if you have a chance of assisting at an elopement, no one could expect you to be particular as to time. Do you really think,' insinuatingly, ' that it is quite right and safe for you to be travelling alone ?'

' I am quite sure that I shall not take you with me. But, Jack, you are not going to see your brother, are you? Because I would rather that he did not know that I had left until . . . until he goes back to Stansfield.'

' My dear Virginia, this looks very bad ;' and Jack seated himself on a truck, and began idly swinging his legs to and fro, with a more serious look upon his boyish countenance than it had worn before. ' You know, all along I begged you not to get married. Why were you in such a

hurry? You might have waited for me.
I always admired you. But, all the same,
I don't approve of you. " Marry in haste,
and repent at leisure." That is all very
well; but you are repenting in such a
hurry. It is all very fine to say you are
not running away; but, at any rate, you
are going off to France, and Norton is to
know nothing about it until he returns, to
find you gone. I daresay it serves him
perfectly right; but have you thought,
Virginia, that he is not *the man to forgive
this sort of thing?*'

The girl involuntarily pressed her hand
against her heart, so violent was its throbs,
so sharp was the pain that shot through
her. She stood as if turned to stone, too
wretched to make an effort at hiding her
misery from the boy. He was right;
his casual words had forced the convic-
tion upon her, and she could not evade it.
Norton would never forgive her. She had
for ever closed the door of reconciliation

T 2

behind her: and had taken a step which could not be retraced.

'Take my advice and go back again,' cried Jack, watching her.

'Oh! I can *never* go back.' Her voice, low though it was, pierced through the shield of even Jack's unemotional youth, and he began to feel very uncomfortable. What if this little comedy, in which he had been quite ready to play a part, were to turn into the first act of a tragedy?

'And you never know where to have married people; it might be rather serious,' said Jack to himself.

'Oh, yes, you will go back sooner or later,' he cried aloud, encouragingly, only anxious at this moment to bring back some colour to the girl's cheeks. 'Only give Norton a little time and he will come to his senses. He will be frightened when he finds you gone.' Then, with a last attempt at jocularity: 'Did he beat you very hard, Virginia?'

But his words fell unheeded. She had not heard him. Her eyes were fixed upon the red lights of an approaching train ; its rush was in her ears. A dreadful terror had taken possession of her senses. What had she done? What was she doing?

She had forgotten Jack's presence, and Mademoiselle Joseph, and it was only the boy's fingers crushing her cold ones in a rough clasp which recalled her to herself.

'Well, if you must and will go, Virginia, I will see you to Dover.'

And it was Jack who, with forethought beyond his years, took tickets and saw to Mademoiselle Joseph's comfort, put her into the train at the right moment, and forced some hot wine and water upon Virginia.

'It is to keep up your pluck, you know,' he said, persuasively. 'And now,' tucking the rugs round her, 'I should advise you, my dear, to go to sleep. I shall be in the smoking compartment if you want me.'

In fact the responsibility of his new position weighed upon him. ' I may never have another chance of eloping with a married woman,' he thought, regretfully; nevertheless, he recognised the fact that in this instance there was no amusement to be got out of the situation. Virginia's eyes, dark with misery and unshed tears, forbade it, and even if Mademoiselle Joseph could have been ignored he could not escape from them. ' Poor child, perhaps she will have a cry when I am not there to see,' said Master Jack to himself, with unusual seriousness, as he lighted a cigar, and not even the indulgence of this strictly forbidden pleasure could divert his thoughts.

In the meantime, through the rush of the train, and Mademoiselle Joseph's murmured observations, through all the bustle of the platform at Dover, the clamour of the porters, and her own mechanical answers to questions about luggage and destination, even on the pier along which Jack was guiding Mademoiselle Joseph's trembling footsteps, whilst, laden with shawls, she followed in their wake; yes, even above the familiar dash of the waves, and the noise of water in the paddle-wheels, she heard Jack still crying,

'He is not the man to forgive this sort of thing, Virginia;' and, alas! she knew that Jack was right.

Just at the last moment the boy walked across the bridge, and as she stood by the vessel's side, looking down at the water through the chill gathering dusk, he flung his arms about her and pressed his cheek to hers.

'Keep up your courage, Virginia,' he cried in his cracked whisper. 'It will be all right. You will have to forgive him; only when Johnny comes marching home mind you let me know.'

And then there was a shout and a whistle and some one pushed him hastily off the deck, and the ship trembled beneath her feet, and she was leaving England and Norton behind her.

In the meantime Norton, amidst many distractions and anxieties of all kinds, had attained to a clearer and more reasonable understanding of how matters really stood between himself and his young wife. His last words to her seemed to him words of madness. He had waited so patiently and so long, surely he might have waited a little longer. What possible good could have been gained by that sudden burst of long-repressed feeling? and now looking back upon it all calmly it seemed to him that her coldness had been assumed; after all, could he be expected to understand all the mysteries of a young girl's heart, he especially who knew so little of women. No wonder if he had frightened her. Then

who could tell what machinations migh
not have been going on against him ; even
if Emmeline were neutral, his step-mother
was an avowed and irritated enemy. It
made him restless to feel that he had left
Virginia in their power. Who could tell
how they might poison her mind against
him.

When after a wearisome day he came
back to his hotel to find Hartley flushed
and sullen sitting over the fire with a cigar
and a French novel, and told him shortly
what he had been able to accomplish on
his behalf, he was merely conscious of a
desire to fulfil a disagreeable task and
return to Stansfield with as little delay as
possible.

' I have done my best. I can only trust
that there are no more bills in the background,' he said, as he laid a pile of papers
upon the table. ' Remember I can do no
more. There is sufficient ready money to
last you for the present. I shall inform

your mother where you are, but you cannot be received at Stansfield.'

Hartley thanked him; though somewhat ungraciously. He could not but be aware that he had got off more easily than he deserved; but his old antagonism towards his brother was only dormant; suppressed for the time by an uneasy sense of gratitude.

' I know it is not everyone that would have done as you have,' he muttered.

But Norton had all an Englishman's dislike to thanks; he looked at his watch and saw that he had just time to catch the last train to Stansfield. He was glad that he had no opportunity to write and apprise them of his coming. He was glad to take Virginia unawares. Perhaps even now he might see in her surprised eyes a gladness which she would have no time to conceal.

It was already past nine o'clock when he arrived at his own door, and, as he stood waiting for his ring to be answered,

a memory of another return at the same
hour was flashed upon his mind, when in
the moonlit garden coming suddenly upon
her he had first taken her in his arms and
told her of his love. So thinking he made
no answer to the surprised looks of the
servant who admitted him, but passing by
the drawing-room door he rapidly mounted
the stairs and made his way to the little
boudoir where she was accustomed after
dinner to sit with Mademoiselle Joseph.

The small room was empty, and in
darkness.

'Virginia,' he cried; but no one answered
him. He struck a light, and with increasing
amazement surveyed its emptiness. Everything was in order but the tables were
bare of all the little trifles which belong
to feminine occupation; the fire had not
accidentally gone out, it had not been
lighted; he opened the door and passed
through his dressing-room to the bed-room
beyond. There too everything was in

dreary and scrupulous order, but Colonel Tennant's photograph had been taken from the wall, and some other little remembrances upon which Virginia placed a special value were missing.

Norton put his candle heavily down upon the table, and looked about him like a man in a dream. What does it all mean? What in this short absence can have taken place? A terrible foreboding of unknown evil falls upon his heart. He hastily retraces his steps, and enters the drawing-room.

'Norton! how you startled me!' and Emmeline rises uttering a cry. 'What a day we have passed here. I must say it was very unkind and inconsiderate of Virginia. Is she with you? Have you seen her?'

'Tell me at once,' cried Norton, turning white. 'I have not seen her. I know nothing.'

'Well! she has not drowned herself, and

that is one comfort. I could never have recovered from such a catastrophe as that in the family. She went off in the most correct way with bag and baggage and Mademoiselle Joseph. Of course mamma had presence of mind not to seem surprised, and gave it out in the house that she had gone to you. She flatters herself that the servants believe it.'

'But where is she? Where can she be?'

Even Emmeline is startled by his tone of anguish, and stares at him in astonishment. He has always appeared to her to be one of the least emotional of men; to whom self-restraint is hardly necessary. What has wrought this change? Incomprehensibly unlikely as it is, is it possible that he is in love with his wife?

'Where is she? How can I tell you?' she answers, querulously. 'Why did you go away and leave her? you might have known that mamma would make mischief, and Virginia had had enough to bear from her already, it was no wonder that she could not stand it any longer. She had too much spirit to complain, still it was not pleasant to be told that you married her because she had run after you in such a manner as to have almost forfeited her character. It was not agreeable to be convicted upon the eaves-dropping testimony of a man like Marshall.'

'And I never knew it. I never heard a word of it until now!'

'No, because she was too proud to tell you. When mamma spoke to her about it, she only laughed. It was not that which really hurt her.'

'What more could have been said?' he cried, with angry bitterness. 'And you knew it, yet you too saw fit to keep silence. But tell me at least what other falsehood malignity could frame. What drove her away?'

'I was not present. I cannot tell you

exactly what passed, and in this case it was the truth, which so often does more damage than a lie. It was the truth, and that was why she could not stand against it. But I know it was a great mistake. Why should she not have been allowed to be happy in her delusion? She fancied, poor child, that you loved her.'

'Yes, yes, go on,' he said, in a rough shaken voice.

'Well, then, you can understand that it was a shock to find that you had married her because when she was ruined you thought that it was the only thing to do for her. Mind, Norton, I do not blame you;' she raised herself, and sat upright in her chair. 'It was a kind act though as it turned out mistaken kindness. She might have seen it herself, only unluckily— she fell in love with you.'

He started visibly, and the rare colour for an instant swept across his features, as, conscious of Emmeline's inquisitive glance, he turned aside hastily, and took a step or two towards the door. If she were right, how blind he had been! But there was hardly room even for this thought in the crowd of conflicting fears which beset him. And for this night at least he could do nothing but wait, for there was no train until the morning.

Mrs. Stansfield had taken no step to trace the fugitives, she had not even chosen to telegraph to her step-son ; as Emmeline had said, her one idea had been to avoid a scandal in her well-ordered household. But she was wise enough to be aware that he was not likely to take this view of the case. She had no wish to see him, and drew a breath of relief when she heard that he had shut himself up in his own rooms, and echoed his thought, though with very different feelings—nothing could now be done until the morning.

And in the early morning as he stands already dressed, weary, anxious, and still perplexed after his restless night, there is an impatient knocking at his door.

'A telegram for you, sir.'

He takes it in silence, but his hand is not quite steady. He glances at the address and almost throws it aside in his revulsion of feeling. It is only from Eton, only from Jack. But he looks at it again and reads:

'*Virginia is well and in safety. You may communicate with her through me.*'

Norton throws down the paper and breaks into a laugh of nervous relief.

'She was right,' he says to himself. 'That is a bad boy. This message was never prompted by Virginia, but all the same I thank him for it, and he shall not be the loser.'

A few hours later, in his master's room at Eton, he was questioning the boy, who, summoned from his studies on the plea of urgent business, had done his best by exasperating evasions to prolong the interview. Now at last the main facts of the case had transpired, and Norton, relieved from his first anxieties, yet remained uneasy and displeased, absently turning over the leaves of a book upon the table near which he stood, whilst Jack, no whit disconcerted, pursued his monologue.

'I always advised her not to marry you,' he was saying. 'I never thought it would turn out well, and now see how right I was. But she always would have her own way, and you will find that she will do as she pleases now. Of course, I begged her to come back; I did not want to have a scandal in the family, I consider it very bad form; but no,' cried Jack, drawing cheerfully upon his imagination, 'nothing made any impression upon her. Though she had only a few shillings in her purse when the tickets were taken, and could not know where any more were to come from, she would go. Well!' sighing heavily, 'I did my best.'

'I suppose Mademoiselle Joseph had some money,' cried Norton, as if awaking from a dream. 'What childish madness . .' and then seeing the boy's small eyes fixed upon him with a gleam of expectancy in them, he stopped suddenly, aware of the absurdity of venting his anger before him.

There was a momentary silence, whilst he walked away to the window with an effort mastering his irritation, and then he heard Jack speaking in somewhat altered tones.

'I say, Norton. Don't you be too hard upon her. After all, it was not her fault that you married her, and it is rough upon her now if she finds out her mistake. You ought to be good to her now that her father is dead and she has no one but you ; and I don't see why you should not be fond of her. I,' impartially, 'I am awfully fond of Virginia.'

'What on earth are you talking about?'

cried Norton, suddenly turning round upon him; and then at the sight of his self-constituted mentor crouched up upon a chair with his knees drawn up to his chin, and a look of genuine anxiety in his inquisitive grey eyes, in spite of his heavy trouble he laughed outright.

'She is unaccountably fond of you,' he muttered; and then, as he prepared to take his departure: 'You must have spent a good deal of money in my service, Jack.'

'We can settle our accounts when you have made it up with Virginia,' answered Jack, loftily, for once indifferent to immediate gains.

But Norton, as he journeyed back to London, had no idea of doing anything in haste. Relieved from immediate anxiety by Jack's communications, he sent off a cheque to Mademoiselle Joseph, and determined for the present to take no further step. Virginia had chosen to separate herself from him; and now he on his part would put her to the proof. He would give her a little breathing-space, at least a few days, to consider and understand what she had done, and to weigh the consequences of the ill-advised step which she had taken. Over and over again Emmeline's words recurred to his memory, 'The poor child fell in love with you.' Was she, could she by any possibility be right? On the answer to that question there hung, so it appeared to him, the happiness of their two lives, and he would not with rash precipitation demand an answer. He remembered how when he had asked her to marry him she had said that it was 'too soon.' She had been right. Now it only remained to be seen if his error might not be retrieved, and this time, at least, he would not err for want of self-control. She had left no word for him, and he would not write to her, but after a few days he would seek her in her old home, and then at last he would have his answer—he would put her to the test.

So his calmer judgment determined; but he would not return to Stansfield. He told himself it was because he would not hear his step-mother's comments upon his wife's conduct, or meet Emmeline's questions; it truth, it was because he would not again enter those doors from which Virginia had gone out; because he would not occupy the old dark rooms into which she had so often brought him the sunshine of her presence; because he dreaded the sight of the lawns across which her light footsteps had passed, and of the shrubberies where she had walked with her hand close clasped in his.

' Virginia, my little love,' he cried to himself, ' why would you not be patient ? Even if you had not loved me at first, in the end I should have made you happy.'

Then, after three days had passed, he found that he could wait no longer, and he started on his journey.

CHAPTER XVI.

MADEMOISELLE JOSEPH sat before the wood-
fire in the little 'salon' at La Vallière,
vainly endeavouring to warm her wrinkled
hands at its blaze. She was chilled and
weary, not yet recovered from all the excitement of the hurried journey; nevertheless, every now and then she looked round
with satisfaction at her well-loved and
familiar surroundings. The bright square
of carpet on the polished floor, the fes-
tooned muslin curtains, the cheerful paper
of trailing dog-roses, the sight of the old
servant in her white cap, who passed in or
out upon one pretence or another to ask
questions and give her news of her old ac-
quaintances in the village. Yes, England

was a beautiful country, but the old Frenchwoman had never felt at home there. She was very glad to be once more in France, in her native village, where she knew everyone's family history, where even she, poor, despised, middle-aged Mademoiselle Joseph, was a person of some importance.

She had almost forgotten the troubles which were threatening her in the future, and her connivance at Virginia's unauthorised journey; and, as to the practical difficulties of the case, did she not hold, closely hidden in her old morocco purse, a letter and an enclosure which might easily solve them all?

'Is it not good to be at home again?' she said, in pleased accents, turning her head round to Virginia; but she gained nothing by the movement, for the girl was standing with her back towards her looking out of the window, and she neither stirred nor answered.

Was this indeed the happy home of her childhood? Her eye wandered over the lawn, with its untended flower-beds, and down the little avenue of limes, whose yellow leaves were blown about in the autumnal wind. And thinking of those vanished years, whose enchantment had for ever fled, tears filled her eyes and rolled unheeded down her cheeks.

'Is it not good to be at home again?' repeated Mademoiselle Joseph. 'Are you not happy, Virginia?'

'Shall I ever be happy again?' she said, despairingly, to herself; but she brushed away her tears, and answered gaily, though she still kept her face turned to the window. 'That is too bold a question. It does not deserve an answer, and it is quite unnecessary besides. Do you not know that it always made me happy to have my own way, and was it not my own wish to come here?'

Yet she would not face any further

questions. What could she say? She
went into the hall, and, catching up a
rough shawl which lay upon the table,
she wrapped it about her, and stepped out
into the garden. A soft wind was blowing up from the west, where, upon the low
line of the horizon, a long streak of prim-
rose light lay beneath a bank of purple
cloud. It played about her uncovered
head, and brought a tinge of colour to her
cheeks, and dried the tears in her sad eyes;
but could not lighten the oppression which
lay upon her heart. How could she, even
in the first mad moment of revolt against
her fate, have imagined that she could live
without him? What if he had not married her for love? Could she doubt that
he was fond of her; that he had, as he
said, liked her from the first? Could she
refuse to believe in the kindness of his
words, his looks, his actions? How many
were the trivial, yet all-convincing evi-
dences of his affection which she could

not but recall? And how had she repaid
his trust? What a blow she had dealt to
his pride and to his confidence.

During the last stormy night, as she lay
through the long hours tossing, in feverish
misery, upon her bed, how often those
words of her boy cousin had repeated
themselves within her heart: 'He is not
the man to forgive.' He will never forgive
her.

'I can never ask it, never,' she says to
herself, in a sob of dull despair.

There was an old stone bench in a recess
of the shrubbery beside the gate. It had
been the little sanctuary of her childhood.
Here she had come to sob out her rare
childish passions; here she had hidden her
dearest treasures, and sought a solitary
hiding-place in moments of keenest joy or
grief; and some sudden freak of memory
has led her to it now. She sinks down
upon the low seat, and buries her face in
her hands.

She does not heed the blustering wind as it whirls the dead leaves about her; she has no thought of the darkening sky, and takes no note of time, as in mournful retrospect she recalls the happiest hours of her short wedded life; those days of pleasant wanderings through foreign towns, of leisurely loiterings in the sunshine, of fresh surprises which his care had designed, proofs of affection hardly heeded at the time, of which the remembrance now strikes with a keen pang upon her heart. Once more she crouches down upon her low seat and bows her head in her hands.

'Virginia, what are you doing here?' asked a grave voice at her elbow.

She started up and the heavy shawl fell back from her shoulders. The wind lifted the masses of brown hair upon her brow; her sad, startled eyes looked up at him; pale, trembling, and wearied by long weeping and sleepless nights, was this the light-hearted girl he had married only a

few weeks ago? But not for an instant
will he allow the shock of this first meeting
to overpower his self-control.

'It is far too cold for you to be out,'
he continued, seriously. 'Can Mademoiselle Joseph take no better care of
you? Let us go in.'

Still Virginia never spoke a word.
Despair and hope strove in a desperate
conflict within her. There was no forgiveness in the studied coldness of his
greeting, no relenting in the calm glance
which met hers; he was too self-possessed
to show any emotion, and, alas! too indifferent to be angry; and yet, if not for
the purpose of reconciliation, for what
purpose had he come?

Silently she turned and led the way
back into the house. He took her shawl
from her in the hall, and, following her
into a little matted room which opened
out of it, he shut the door behind him.
The slight window-frames shook in the

wind; the loosened creepers were blown against the panes; outside there was the prospect of the dank lawn, the bending laurels, and the cloud-swept sky.

'So this is La Vallière,' observed Norton, regarding it.

'It does not seem the same,' cried Virginia, speaking eagerly and for the first time. 'Yes, I know what I told you, but it was true. I thought no place on earth was like it; but I see now, I understand, it was because I was happy here.'

'Why should you not be happy here again? Why should you so soon despair?' he answered, smiling coldly. 'Perhaps you are afraid that I may interfere with your happiness, but, believe me, I have no wish to do so. I hoped, yes, you knew it, I hoped to make you happy, but you have given me the strongest proof in your power of my absolute, irrevocable failure. I should be mad indeed to refuse to believe you.'

She had sunk down upon a chair, and, resting her elbow on the table, she shaded her eyes with her hand and looked down at its polished surface; yet at this cruellest moment of her pain her courage had not deserted her; she could at least suffer in silence, since she could no longer escape from the knowledge that her forebodings were all too true, and Mrs. Stansfield's suggestions but too well founded. Already after these few weeks he repented his hasty generosity, he was glad to catch at the opportunity which her rash conduct had afforded him to release himself from the constant daily pressure of a tie from which he could not now be free. It was not for her to withstand his will; and yet what had brought him here? and involuntarily she cried under her breath:

'Why did you come?'

'Is that such a difficult question to answer?' He was standing now as far from her as possible in the narrow limits of the room leaning against the low chimney-piece with his back to the empty grate. 'You surely did not suppose that I thought myself relieved from all responsibilities regarding you, and you left me no time, no chance to make the necessary arrangements. It is true this house is your own, as I told you before, but——' suddenly looking down at her with his keen searching glance—'what did you propose to do?'

The colour rushed to her cheeks; the burning tears sprang to her eyes.

'I had not thought. I had had no time.'

'That is your excuse,' he said, more softly. 'But had you not time to remember that you married me of your own free will only a few weeks ago? What had I done, Virginia, to alienate the affection which at least you professed to feel? what had I done to forfeit your trust?'

'Nothing,' she cried, as if the word was wrung from her against her will. 'Nothing.'

'Then let me echo your own words; why did you come here?'

'They told me . . . it had been a mistake . . that you were only sorry for me. Aunt Charlotte said so and Emmeline believed it, they said . . .'

'And are they to come between us?' he asked, with growing displeasure. 'Can you so soon have forgotten your promises? Well,' after a silence which she made no effort to break, 'if it must be so you shall have your way; and do not imagine that my anger against you will last for ever. I shall forgive you, I shall not find it so easy to forgive myself; but at any rate I did it in ignorance; I did not imagine . .'

'What?' she asked, for an instant lifting her head.

'I did not imagine that you would so soon discover that anything was better than to remain with me. When I brought you back to Stansfield, Virginia, I had hoped that it might be your home; and a happy one.'

'I was happy,' she murmured.

'Yes, for a few days,' he answered, bitterly. 'It must be my endeavour now to ensure you as far as I can a more safe and enduring happiness.'

'Here at La Vallière?' she questioned, quickly; and the next instant would have given worlds to recall her words.

It was all over; he would not offer to take her back with him. His affection was alienated and such love as he had once had for her was cold and dead.

'Where else would you wish to be? But no doubt it requires consideration; do not answer at once. I too have much to consider. I will see you again presently; when I have spoken to Mademoiselle Joseph.'

A few minutes later, as he sat by the old lady's side, he was saying, gloomily,

'I believe you were all mistaken. Poor

child, she was glad of any excuse to escape.
I made a mistake, she was too young.
Nevertheless, I cannot leave her here, even
if she desired it, except for a time. For
the present, perhaps it may be best.'

'Then she does not know that you had
come to take her back?' asked Mademoiselle
Joseph, nervously folding and unfolding her
pocket-handkerchief.

'She gave me no encouragement to tell
her;' and his brow darkened at the remembrance of her startled silent greeting. 'I
shall say nothing which would force her to
return; only if she remains, even for a
time, I must make some arrangement.'

'But the money you have already sent
is far too large a sum;' and Mademoiselle
Joseph began to fumble with her pocket-
book. 'I am afraid to sleep with it in
the house, and Virginia knows nothing of
it. I have not dared to tell her.'

'It is not necessary,' he answered. But
after a time he got up restlessly, and

walked out into the passage. He said to himself that the test he had applied had been a fair one. He had come upon her suddenly, and how had she received him? with manifest trembling, with silent averted looks, with faltering excuses for a step of whose real significance in his eyes she appeared to have no conception. He did not think that she intended to deceive him, and yet could he believe that there was not some feeling in the background which Mrs. Stansfield's words had but forced into action. Virginia was not just, but he did not blame her for that; it was natural, perhaps, that she should exact from him what she had not to give, and he was even glad that she should exact it; at least, he had avoided one error, he had not wearied her with his love, he had been her friend rather than her lover, and yet she had chafed under the tie which bound her to him. She was too young, as he had said, and she had struggled to be free. Now, remembering her cold, constrained, and almost fearful greeting he could not but also remember that she had in these last days sent him no word, asked no forgiveness. No, she did not know what love was, she had never loved him. And yet he could not leave her now in silence. It might be best, but he could not do it. He stopped in his walk and pushed open the door of the room where he had left her.

The dusk had already fallen, and he could but dimly discern the outline of her figure as she sat still where he had left her, half-an-hour ago. Her arms were outspread in an attitude of deepest dejection upon the table, and she had laid her head down upon them.

' It is all over,' she said to herself in her despair, whilst sobs shook her slight frame and tears fell like rain over her pale cheeks and clasped hands. ' He never loved me. He is glad to be free. I am his wife, he

cannot help that, and he means to do his
duty, but he does not want to be with me.
He does not even like me any longer.
Why did I marry him? Oh! Norton,
Norton, why did you let me do it?'

As unconsciously she breathed out the
last words, she suddenly caught her
breath. Absorbed by her grief she had
not heard him softly open the door, but
now a sudden sense of some near presence
startled her into silence.

'Virginia,' he said. 'Tell me, let us at
least understand one another. What is
your complaint!'

'Why did you let me marry you?' she
said, and she lifted her head and pushed
back the hair from her brow. Her misery
is too great for her to be conscious of side
issues or afraid of possible misconstructions.
It is a relief to speak, it is impossible to be
silent. 'Yes, why did you let me do it?
I was a child, I did not know—but you
knew what you were doing. You had no

right to ask for what you could not give. Yes, if not in word, over and over again in other ways you asked me if I loved you.'

A burning blush replaced her deadly pallor, and, forgetting that in the dim light it would pass unnoticed, she hid her face once more in her hands.

' And what answer did you make me ?' asked Norton, in tones deepened and lowered by the effort to repress his increasing anxiety. ' What answer could you make ?'

' None. I gave you none because I did not know; I did not understand.'

' Was that the only reason ?' he cried, unsteadily. ' Then now at least the time has come for you to speak plainly.'

He stepped to the fireside and lighted the candles which stood upon the chimney-piece. Their faint, flickering light showed the bare, whitewashed walls, the shabby furniture, the square of the uncurtained window, and the girl's desolate figure, her tear-stained cheeks and sunken eyes.

His heart was stirred within him.   What
if after all they should both have been
mistaken !

He came and knelt down beside her
and laid his hand softly on her ruffled
hair.

'Tell me at last, Virginia,' he cried, under
his breath.   'Do you love me now?'

'You know it.   You know it;' and her
voice broke in sobs.   But when he would
have taken her in his arms she thrust him
away. 'You have no right to ask it.
You ... you knew it long ago.'

'I did not,' he answered, with serious
sincerity.   'And even now I cannot
understand.   Why did you go away from
me?'

'Because they told me . . . .'

'What was false; what never was the
truth.   Oh, Virginia, long ago—before you
knew it yourself—even before you heard
me call you by your name, when no promise had passed between us, when you

were still free—still, as you have said, a child,—I loved you.'

She lifted her head and her blue eyes regarded him long and earnestly. Then suddenly the colour rose in her cheeks and she put her arms about him and hid her face upon her husband's shoulder.

.   .   .   .

'I must go,' she said presently, and withdrew herself from him. 'I must go and tell Mademoiselle Joseph.'

'What will you tell her? That you are sorry, that you were wrong and that I was right: shall not the fairy tale come true, Virginia: they married and were happy ever after?'

'Do not look on,' she cried, quickly, 'I am happy now. Is not that enough?'

'Yes, it is enough;' and a deep content shone in his eyes. 'For one part of the story at least is true;' and he touched the ring upon his wife's finger. Then suddenly:

'Virginia, I am not a forgiving man; how is it that I have so soon forgiven you?'

But she only laughed; standing before him in the little bare room with the old smile upon her lips and a light shining in eyes still wet with tears.

'I must go,' she said, breaking from him. 'I must go and tell Mademoiselle Joseph.'

'Yes, but what shall you tell her? What shall you say?'

'I shall say that we are going home—to Stansfield,' said Virginia.

THE END.

LONDON: PRINTED BY DUNCAN MACDONALD, BLENHEIM HOUSE.

HURST & BLACKETT'S

LIST OF NEW WORKS.

LONDON:

13, GREAT MARLBOROUGH STREET, W.

EDNA LYALL'S NOVELS

EACH IN ONE VOLUME CROWN 8vo, 6s.

KNIGHT-ERRANT.

"'Knight-Errant' is marked by the author's best qualities as a writer of fiction, and displays on every page the grace and quiet power of her former works."—*Athenæum.*

"The plot, and, indeed, the whole story, is gracefully fresh and very charming; there is a wide humanity in the book that cannot fail to accomplish its author's purpose."—*Literary World.*

"This novel is distinctly helpful and inspiring from its high tone, its intense human feeling, and its elevated morality. It forms an additional proof, if such were needed, that Miss Lyall has a mandate to write."—*Academy.*

DONOVAN:

A MODERN ENGLISHMAN.

"This is a very admirable work. The reader is from the first carried away by the gallant unconventionality of its author. 'Donovan' is a very excellent novel; but it is something more and better. It should do as much good as the best sermon ever written or delivered extempore. The story is told with a grand simplicity, an unconscious poetry of eloquence which stirs the very depths of the heart. One of the main excellencies of this novel is the delicacy of touch with which the author shows her most delightful characters to be after all human beings, and not angels before their time."—*Standard.*

WE TWO.

"A work of deep thought and much power. Serious as it is, it is now and then brightened by rays of genuine humour. Altogether this story is more and better than a novel."—*Morning Post.*

"There is artistic realism both in the conception and the delineation of the personages; the action and interest are unflaggingly sustained from first to last, and the book is pervaded by an atmosphere of elevated, earnest thought."—*Scotsman.*

IN THE GOLDEN DAYS.

"Miss Lyall has given us a vigorous study of such life and character as are really worth reading about. The central figure of her story is Algernon Sydney; and this figure she invests with a singular dignity and power. He always appears with effect, but no liberties are taken with the facts of his life. The plot is adapted with great felicity to them. His part in it, absolutely consistent as it is with historical truth, gives it reality as well as dignity. Some of the scenes are remarkably vivid. The escape is an admirable narrative, which almost makes one hold one's breath as one reads."—*Spectator.*

WON BY WAITING.

"The Dean's daughters are perfectly real characters—the learned Cornelia especially; —the little impulsive French heroine, who endures their cold hospitality and at last wins their affection, is thoroughly charming; while throughout the book there runs a golden thread of pure brotherly and sisterly love, which pleasantly reminds us that the making and marring of marriage is not, after all, the sum total of real life."—*Academy.*

LONDON : HURST AND BLACKETT, LIMITED.

2

MESSRS. HURST AND BLACKETT'S
LIST OF NEW WORKS.

BANDOBAST AND KHABAR; REMINISCENCES OF
INDIA. By COLONEL CUTHBERT LARKING. With twelve Illustrations,
from original Drawings by the Author. 1 vol. small 4to. 10s. 6d.

"The author's accounts of tiger hunts will be entertaining both to those who
have met and those who desire to meet the king of the Indian fauna in his own
dominions."—*Morning Post.*
"Colonel Larking is to be the more congratulated on having written a readable work of travel in an already well-known country."—*Society Herald.*

REMINISCENCES OF ETON (KEATE'S TIME).
By the REV. C. ALLIX WILKINSON, M.A., Author of "Remini-
scences of the Court and Times of King Ernest of Hanover."
With Portrait of Dr. Keate. 1 vol. crown 8vo. 6s.

"Mr. Wilkinson's book is thoroughly fresh and entertaining; it is crammed
full of good stories, and will be a joy to all Etonians."—*Graphic.*

LADY HAMILTON AND LORD NELSON. An
Historical Biography based on Letters and other Documents in
the possession of ALFRED MORRISON, Esq., of Fonthill, Wiltshire.
By JOHN CORDY JEAFFRESON, Author of "The real Lord Byron,"
&c. 2 vols. crown 8vo. 21s.

"Mr. Jeaffreson may be thanked for the new and favourable light which he has
been able to throw upon the public and private conduct both of Lady Hamilton
and of Nelson."—*Globe.*
"It only remains for us to compliment Mr. Jeaffreson upon the reliable, painstaking, thorough way in which he has dealt with the story of Lady Hamilton,
without offending the moral sense of his readers."—*Academy.*

FOUR MONTHS' CRUISE IN A SAILING
YACHT. By LADY ERNESTINE EDGCUMBE and LADY MARY
WOOD. With Illustrations. 1 vol. crown 8vo. 7s. 6d.

"The whole journey is recounted in such a way as to make the narrative
agreeable reading, and to intending travellers in the same track it contains many
useful hints and suggestions."—*The Queen.*

RECORDS OF SERVICE AND CAMPAIGNING
IN MANY LANDS. By SURGEON-GENERAL MUNRO, M.D., C.B.,
Author of "Reminiscences of Military Service with the 93rd
Sutherland Highlanders," &c. DEDICATED BY PERMISSION TO
H. R. H. THE PRINCESS LOUISE. 2 vols. crown 8vo. 21s.

"The story which Dr. Munro has to tell is one which never flags or ceases to
be instructive as well as interesting."—*Spectator.*
"These Records should be in the hands of every soldier, for the sake of the
information which they give and the spirit which informs them."—*Globe.*
"Full of interesting notes on the army and army life."—*Graphic.*

EIGHTEENTH CENTURY WAIFS. By JOHN
ASHTON, Author of 'Social Life in the Reign of Queen Anne,' &c.
1 vol. small 4to. 12s.

"The matter contained in this book is always pleasing and instructive. There
is certainly not a dull page in the volume."—*Globe.*
"Mr. Ashton has produced a volume of light and pleasant character."—*Morning
Post.*

SHIKAR SKETCHES: WITH NOTES ON INDIAN

FIELD SPORTS. By J. MORAY BROWN, late 79th Cameron Highlanders. With Eight Illustrations, by J. C. DOLLMAN, R.I. 1 vol. small 4to. 10s. 6d.

"A glorious book. It is palpably the work of a true sportsman."—*Horse and Hound.*
"The Sketches are delightfully written, models of clear, bright, racy narrative, and containing just those particulars that a sportsman wishes to know.'—*Scotsman.*
"The author goes through the round of Indian sport, and writes in such a pleasant fashion as to make his pages agreeable reading to all for whom the subject itself has attractions; the book has the additional advantage of some spirited illustrations."—*The Field.*
"Mr. Moray Brown records his long experiences among big game in India with capital spirit and style; there are some thrilling pages on pig-sticking and tiger-shooting."—*The World.*

THROUGH CYPRUS. By AGNES SMITH, Author

of "Glimpses of Greek Life and Scenery," &c. 1 vol. demy 8vo. With Illustrations and Map of the Author's Route. 15s.

"The cheerful and observant authoress has much that is new to tell us."—*Daily Telegraph.*
"'Through Cyprus' may be heartily commended to readers who are fond of an entertaining and chatty narration of incidents of travel."—*Scotsman.*

REMINISCENCES OF THE COURT AND

TIMES OF KING ERNEST OF HANOVER. By the Rev. C. A. WILKINSON, M.A., His Majesty's Resident Domestic Chaplain. *Second and Cheaper Edition.* 1 vol. crown 8vo. With portrait of the King. 6s.

"Mr. Wilkinson's descriptions of the Court balls, where even the ladies took precedence according to military rank, of the characters he met with, and of the Hanoverian clergy of those days, will be found decidedly interesting."—*Spectator.*
"An interesting book, which abounds in characteristic stories of the old king, in anecdotes of many celebrities, English and foreign, of the early part of this century, and, indeed, of all kinds and conditions of men and women with whom the author was brought in contact by his courtly or pastoral office."—*St. James's Gazette.*

THE LIFE AND ADVENTURES OF PEG

WOFFINGTON: WITH PICTURES OF THE PERIOD IN WHICH SHE LIVED. By J. FITZGERALD MOLLOY, Author of "Court Life Below Stairs," &c. *Third and Cheaper Edition.* 1 vol. crown 8vo. With Portrait. 6s.

"Peg Woffington makes a most interesting central figure, round which Mr. Molloy has made to revolve a varied and picturesque panorama of London life in the middle of the 18th century. He sees things in the past so clearly, grasps them so tenaciously, and reproduces them so vividly that they come to us without any of the dust and rust of time."—*G. A. S. in the Illustrated London News.*
"Mr. Molloy's work has the merit at least of being from the first chapter to the last without a single dull page."—*Daily News.*

CHAPTERS FROM FAMILY CHESTS. By

EDWARD WALFORD, M.A., Author of 'The County Families,' &c. 2 vols. crown 8vo. 21s.

"'Chapters from Family Chests' are a great deal more exciting and absorbing than one half the professedly sensational novels."—*Daily Telegraph.*
"Mr. Walford's volumes abound in what is known as the romance of real life, and are extremely interesting reading."—*Daily News.*

THE EGYPTIAN CAMPAIGNS, 1882 TO 1885,

AND THE EVENTS WHICH LED TO THEM. By CHARLES ROYLE, Barrister-at-Law, of ALEXANDRIA. 2 vols. demy 8vo. Illustrated by Maps and Plans. 30s.

"Mr. Royle has done well in the interests of historical completeness to describe not only the entire military drama, but also the political events connected with it, and whoever reads the book with care has gone a considerable way towards mastering the difficult Egyptian question."—*Athenæum.*

"The Egyptian fiasco has found in Mr. Royle a most painstaking, accurate, and judicious historian. From a literary point of view his volumes may be thought to contain too many unimportant incidents, yet their presence was necessary perhaps, in a complete record, and the most fastidious reader will acquit Mr. Royle of filling his pages with anything that can be called padding."—*St. James's Gazette.*

FOOTSTEPS OF JEANNE D'ARC. A Pilgrimage.

By Mrs. FLORENCE CADDY. 1 vol. demy 8vo. With Map of Route. 15s.

"The reader, whatever his preconceived notions of the maid may have been, will soon find himself in sympathy with a writer who, by the charm of her descriptive style, at once arrests his attention and sustains the interest of her subject."—*Morning Post.*

THE FRIENDSHIPS OF MARY RUSSELL

MITFORD: AS RECORDED IN LETTERS FROM HER LITERARY CORRESPONDENTS. Edited by the REV. A. G. L'ESTRANGE, Editor of "The Life of Mary Russell Mitford," &c. 2 vols. 21s.

"These letters are all written as to one whom the writers love and revere. Miss Barrett is one of Miss Mitford's correspondents, all of whom seem to be inspired with a sense of excellence in the mind they are invoking. Their letters are extremely interesting, and they strike out recollections, opinions, criticisms, which will hold the reader's delighted and serious attention."—*Daily Telegraph.*

THE BRONTË FAMILY, With Special Reference

to PATRICK BRANWELL BRONTE. By FRANCIS A. LEYLAND. 2 vols. 21s.

"This book is so full of interesting information that as a contribution to literary biography it may be considered a real success."—*Academy.*

"Mr. Leyland's book is earnest and accurate, and he has spared no pains to master his subject and present it with clearness; the book is valuable, and should be read by all who are familiar with the previous works on the family."—*Graphic.*

MEMOIRS OF A CAMBRIDGE CHORISTER.

By WILLIAM GLOVER. 2 vols. crown 8vo. 21s.

"In these amusing volumes Mr. Glover provides us with the means of spending a pleasant hour or two in his company."—*Times.*

"These volumes contain a miscellaneous set of reminiscences, comments, and anecdotes, written in a light and jocular style. Mr. Glover is always cheerful and never didactic."—*Athenæum.*

WITHOUT GOD: NEGATIVE SCIENCE AND NATURAL

ETHICS. By PERCY GREG, Author of "The Devil's Advocate," "Across the Zodiac," &c. 1 vol. demy 8vo. 12s.

"Mr. Greg has condensed much profound thought into his book, and has fully succeeded in maintaining the interest of the discussion throughout."—*Morning Post.*

"This work is ably written; there are in it many passages of no ordinary power and brilliancy. It is eminently suggestive and stimulating."—*Scotsman.*

PLAIN SPEAKING. By Author of "John Halifax,

Gentleman." 1 vol. crown 8vo. 6s.

"We recommend 'Plain Speaking' to all who like amusing, wholesome, and instructive reading. The contents of Mrs. Craik's volume are of the most multifarious kind, but all the papers are good and readable, and one at least of them of real importance."—*St. James's Gazette.*

𝔘nder the 𝔈special 𝔓atronage of 𝔥er 𝔐ajesty.

Published annually, in One Vol., royal 8vo, with the Arms beautifully engraved, handsomely bound, with gilt edges, price 31s. 6d.

LODGE'S PEERAGE
AND BARONETAGE,
CORRECTED BY THE NOBILITY.

FIFTY-SEVENTH EDITION FOR 1888.

LODGE'S PEERAGE AND BARONETAGE is acknowledged to be the most complete, as well as the most elegant, work of the kind. As an established and authentic authority on all questions respecting the family histories, honours, and connections of the titled aristocracy, no work has ever stood so high. It is published under the especial patronage of Her Majesty, and is annually corrected throughout, from the personal communications of the Nobility. It is the only work of its class in which, *the type being kept constantly standing*, every correction is made in its proper place to the date of publication, an advantage which gives it supremacy over all its competitors. Independently of its full and authentic information respecting the existing Peers and Baronets of the realm, the most sedulous attention is given in its pages to the collateral branches of the various noble families, and the names of many thousand individuals are introduced, which do not appear in other records of the titled classes. For its authority, correctness, and facility of arrangement, and the beauty of its typography and binding, the work is justly entitled to the place it occupies on the tables of Her Majesty and the Nobility.

LIST OF THE PRINCIPAL CONTENTS.

Historical View of the Peerage.
Parliamentary Roll of the House of Lords.
English, Scotch, and Irish Peers, in their orders of Precedence.
Alphabetical List of Peers of Great Britain and the United Kingdom, holding superior rank in the Scotch or Irish Peerage.
Alphabetical list of Scotch and Irish Peers, holding superior titles in the Peerage of Great Britain and the United Kingdom.
A Collective list of Peers, in their order of Precedence.
Table of Precedency among Men.
Table of Precedency among Women.
The Queen and the Royal Family.
Peers of the Blood Royal.
The Peerage, alphabetically arranged.
Families of such Extinct Peers as have left Widows or Issue.
Alphabetical List of the Surnames of all the Peers.

The Archbishops and Bishops of England and Ireland.
The Baronetage alphabetically arranged.
Alphabetical List of Surnames assumed by members of Noble Families.
Alphabetical List of the Second Titles of Peers, usually borne by their Eldest Sons.
Alphabetical Index to the Daughters of Dukes, Marquises, and Earls, who, having married Commoners, retain the title of Lady before their own Christian and their Husband's Surnames.
Alphabetical Index to the Daughters of Viscounts and Barons, who, having married Commoners, are styled Honourable Mrs.; and, in case of the husband being a Baronet or Knight, Hon. Lady.
A List of the Orders of Knighthood.
Mottoes alphabotically arranged and translated.

"This work is the most perfect and elaborate record of the living and recently deceased members of the Peerage of the Three Kingdoms as it stands at this day. It is a most useful publication. We are happy to bear testimony to the fact that scrupulous accuracy is a distinguishing feature of this book."—*Times.*

"Lodge's Peerage must supersede all other works of the kind, for two reasons: first, it is on a better plan; and secondly, it is better executed. We can safely pronounce it to be the readiest, the most useful, and exactest of modern works on the subject."—*Spectator:*

"A work of great value. It is the most faithful record we possess of the aristocracy of the day."—*Post.*

THE NEW AND POPULAR NOVELS.
PUBLISHED BY HURST & BLACKETT.

THE GOLDEN HOPE: A ROMANCE OF THE DEEP.
By W. CLARK RUSSELL, Author of "A Sea Queen," "The Wreck of the Grosvenor," &c. 1 vol. 6s.
"Mr. Clark Russell is at his best in 'The Golden Hope,' which means that this book of his is one of the finest books of its kind in our language."—*Academy.*

A HOUSE PARTY. By OUIDA. *(Second Edition.)*
1 vol. crown 8vo. 6s.
"The sketches of character are hit off with accuracy of observation and with a firm and clear outline."—*Daily Telegraph.*

ON THE SCENT. By LADY MARGARET MAJENDIE,
Author of 'Dita,' 'Once More,' 'Sisters-in-Law,' &c. 1 vol. crown 8vo. 6s.
"A bright and wholesome story."—*St. James's Gazette.*

IN BAD HANDS. By F. W. ROBINSON, Author
of "Grandmother's Money," "The Courting of Mary Smith," &c. 3 vols.
"The volumes are alive with touches of humour and pathos, and are pretty sure to be welcomed by novel-readers."—*Athenæum*

THE TREASURE OF THORBURNS. A Novel.
By FREDERICK BOYLE, Author of "A Good Hater," "Legends of my Bungalow," &c. 3 vols.
"The story is excellent in its way, more than sufficiently well written, and with certain touches of fresh originality that lift it out of the pale of the commonplace."—*Literary World.*

WEEPING FERRY. A Novel. By GEORGE HALSE.
2 vols.
"'Weeping Ferry' is decidedly above the average of contemporary novels."—*Saturday Review.*
"Mr. Halse's pages are simply and prettily written."—*Scotsman.*

COULD HE DO BETTER? By ARTHUR A.
HOFFMANN. 3 vols.
"The writing is throughout careful yet easy, never tame and never affected, and the structure of the story has compactness, proportion, and symmetry."—*Spectator.*

THE SON OF HIS FATHER. By Mrs. OLIPHANT,
Author of "It was a Lover and his Lass," "Agnes," &c. 3 vols.
"No previous work of Mrs. Oliphant better justifies her high position among English novelists than her new book. It is difficult to speak too highly of the truth, power, and pathos of this tale."—*Morning Post.*

CATERINA. By the Author of "Lauterdale." 3 vols.
"The author is really an able writer, and he has a good grasp of character."—*Academy.*
"A moving and animated story."—*Daily Telegraph.*

CAST ON THE WATERS. By HUGH COLEMAN
DAVIDSON, Author of "The Green Hills by the Sea." 3 vols.
"The every-day events of the tale are all forcibly and graphically portrayed."—*Morning Post.*
"The characters are well drawn in caricaturist's style, and the dialogue apt and amusing."—*Scotsman.*

7

THE NEW AND POPULAR NOVELS.
PUBLISHED BY HURST & BLACKETT.

VIRGINIA TENNANT. By the Author of "Christina North," "A Golden Bar," &c. 2 vols.

ONLY A CORAL GIRL. By GERTRUDE FORDE, Author of "Driven Before the Storm," &c. 3 vols.

A FAIR CRUSADER; A STORY OF TO-DAY. By WILLIAM WESTALL, Author of "Larry Lohengrin," "A Queer Race," &c. 2 vols.

A BRETON MAIDEN. By A FRENCH LADY, Author of "Till my Wedding-Day." 3 vols.

"Time and space alike would fail us to note the many fine points of this admirable novel."—*Academy.*

"The author's local colouring is always good, and she has perfectly caught the spirit of the time she depicts."—*Morning Post.*

BORN IN THE PURPLE. By MAXWELL FOX. 3 vols.

"'Born in the Purple' is not wanting in originality, and on the whole is free from the reproach of dulness."—*Morning Post.*

A NEW FACE AT THE DOOR. By JANE STANLEY, Author of "A Daughter of the Gods." 2 vols.

"All the characters are well described, the young people being drawn with a clever hand, and standing out distinctly in their several ways as real persons."—*Queen.*

"The tone of the whole book is natural and healthy, and it is pleasant reading."—*Saturday Review.*

THE SPORT OF CHANCE. By WILLIAM SHARP. 3 vols.

"'The Sport of Chance' has *prima facie* an undeniable advantage to start with: *i.e.*, it is unlike almost anything hitherto written in the shape of a novel in three volumes. The author shows much skill in unravelling the tangled skein of a complicated plot."—*Morning Post.*

SWEET IS TRUE LOVE. By KATHARINE KING, Author of "The Queen of the Regiment," "Off the Roll," &c. 2 vols.

"It is in the tender sympathetic treatment of details that the writer is most successful."—*St. James's Gazette.*

A DOUBLE WEDDING. By the Author of "St. Olave's," "Janita's Cross," &c. 3 vols.

"The tale is told with quaint and pathetic simplicity, and is in every sense a charming story."—*Morning Post.*

"The work is a combination of refined quiet humour and gentle pathos which produce a delightful whole."—*Whitehall Review.*

THE GAY WORLD. By JOSEPH HATTON, Author of "Clytie," &c. 3 vols.

"The chief characters all have a certain charm. One follows with genuine anxiety the course of their career."—*Globe.*

"The book is interspersed with many clever passages, bits of choice description, and happy touches of character; it is the ablest novel Mr. Hatton has written."—*Academy.*

8

HURST & BLACKETT'S STANDARD LIBRARY

OF CHEAP EDITIONS OF

POPULAR MODERN WORKS.

ILLUSTRATED BY

SIR J. E. MILLAIS, SIR J. GILBERT, HOLMAN HUNT, BIRKET FOSTER, JOHN LEECH, JOHN TENNIEL, J. LASLETT POTT, ETC.

Each in a Single Volume, with Frontispiece, price 5s.

I.—SAM SLICK'S NATURE AND HUMAN NATURE.

"The first volume of Messrs. Hurst and Blackett's Standard Library of Cheap Editions forms a very good beginning to what will doubtless be a very successful undertaking. 'Nature and Human Nature' is one of the best of Sam Slick's witty and humorous productions, and well entitled to the large circulation which it cannot fail to obtain in its present convenient and cheap shape. The volume combines with the great recommendations of a clear, bold type and good paper, the lesser, but attractive merits of being well illustrated and elegantly bound."—*Morning Post.*

II.—JOHN HALIFAX, GENTLEMAN.

"The new and cheaper edition of this interesting work will doubtless meet with great success. John Halifax, the hero of this most beautiful story, is no ordinary hero, and this his history is no ordinary book. It is a full-length portrait of a true gentleman, one of nature's own nobility. It is also the history of a home, and a thoroughly English one. The work abounds in incident, and many of the scenes are full of graphic power and true pathos. It is a book that few will read without becoming wiser and better."—*Scotsman.*

"This story is very interesting. The attachment between John Halifax and his wife is beautifully painted, as are the pictures of their domestic life, and the growing up of their children; and the conclusion of the book is beautiful and touching."—*Athenæum.*

III.—THE CRESCENT AND THE CROSS.

BY ELIOT WARBURTON.

"Independent of its value as an original narrative, and its useful and interesting information, this work is remarkable for the colouring power and play of fancy with which its descriptions are enlivened. Among its greatest and most lasting charms is its reverent and serious spirit."—*Quarterly Review.*

"Mr. Warburton has fulfilled the promise of his title-page. The 'Realities of Eastern Travel' are described with a vividness which invests them with deep and abiding interest; while the 'Romantic' adventures which the enterprising tourist met with in his course are narrated with a spirit which shows how much he enjoyed these reliefs from the ennui of every-day life."—*Globe.*

IV.—NATHALIE.

BY JULIA KAVANAGH.

"'Nathalie' is Miss Kavanagh's best imaginative effort. Its manner is gracious and attractive. Its matter is good. A sentiment, a tenderness, are commanded by her which are as individual as they are elegant. We should not soon come to an end were we to specify all the delicate touches and attractive pictures which place 'Nathalie' high among books of its class."—*Athenæum.*

V.—A WOMAN'S THOUGHTS ABOUT WOMEN.

BY THE AUTHOR OF "JOHN HALIFAX, GENTLEMAN."

"These thoughts are good and humane. They are thoughts we would wish women to think: they are much more to the purpose than the treatises upon the women and daughters of England, which were fashionable some years ago, and these thoughts mark the progress of opinion, and indicate a higher tone of character, and a juster estimate of woman's position."—*Athenæum.*

"This excellent book is characterised by good sense, good taste, and feeling, and is written in an earnest, philanthropic, as well as practical spirit."—*Morning Post.*

HURST & BLACKETT'S STANDARD LIBRARY

VI.—ADAM GRAEME OF MOSSGRAY.

BY MRS. OLIPHANT.

"'Adam Graeme' is a story awakening genuine emotions of interest and delight by its admirable pictures of Scottish life and scenery. The plot is cleverly complicated, and there is great vitality in the dialogue, and remarkable brilliancy in the descriptive passages, as who that has read 'Margaret Maitland' would not be prepared to expect? But the story has a 'mightier magnet still,' in the healthy tone which pervades it, in its feminine delicacy of thought and diction, and in the truly womanly tenderness of its sentiments. The eloquent author sets before us the essential attributes of Christian virtue, their deep and silent workings in the heart, and their beautiful manifestations in the life, with a delicacy, a power, and a truth which can hardly be surpassed."—*Morning Post.*

VII.—SAM SLICK'S WISE SAWS AND MODERN INSTANCES.

"We have not the slightest intention to criticise this book. Its reputation is made, and will stand as long as that of Scott's or Bulwer's novels. The remarkable originality of its purpose, and the happy description it affords of American life and manners, still continue the subject of universal admiration. To say thus much is to say enough, though we must just mention that the new edition forms a part of the Publishers' Cheap Standard Library, which has included some of the very best specimens of light literature that ever have been written."—*Messenger.*

VIII.—CARDINAL WISEMAN'S RECOLLECTIONS OF THE LAST FOUR POPES.

"A picturesque book on Rome and its ecclesiastical sovereigns, by an eloquent Roman Catholic. Cardinal Wiseman has here treated a special subject with so much generality and geniality that his recollections will excite no ill-feeling in those who are most conscientiously opposed to every idea of human infallibility represented in Papal domination."—*Athenæum.*

IX.—A LIFE FOR A LIFE.

BY THE AUTHOR OF "JOHN HALIFAX, GENTLEMAN."

"We are always glad to welcome Mrs. Craik. She writes from her own convictions, and she has the power not only to conceive clearly what it is that she wishes to say, but to express it in language effective and vigorous. In 'A Life for a Life' she is fortunate in a good subject, and she has produced a work of strong effect. The reader, having read the book through for the story, will be apt (if he be of our persuasion) to return and read again many pages and passages with greater pleasure than on a first perusal. The whole book is replete with a graceful, tender delicacy; and, in addition to its other merits, it is written in good careful English."—*Athenæum.*

"'A Life for a Life' is a book of a high class. The characters are depicted with a masterly hand; the events are dramatically set forth; the descriptions of scenery and sketches of society are admirably penned; moreover, the work has an object—a clearly defined moral—most poetically, most beautifully drawn, and through all there is that strong, reflective mind visible which lays bare the human heart and human mind to the very core."—*Morning Post.*

X.—THE OLD COURT SUBURB.

BY LEIGH HUNT.

"A book which has afforded us no slight gratification."—*Athenæum.*

"From the mixture of description, anecdote, biography, and criticism, this book is very pleasant reading."—*Spectator.*

"A more agreeable and entertaining book has not been published since Boswell produced his reminiscences of Johnson."—*Observer.*

10

XI.—MARGARET AND HER BRIDESMAIDS.

BY THE AUTHOR OF "THE VALLEY OF A HUNDRED FIRES."

"We recommend all who are in search of a fascinating novel to read this work for themselves. They will find it well worth their while. There are a freshness and originality about it quite charming, and there is a certain nobleness in the treatment both of sentiment and incident which is not often found."—*Athenæum.*

XII.—THE OLD JUDGE; OR, LIFE IN A COLONY.

BY SAM SLICK.

"A peculiar interest attaches to sketches of colonial life, and readers could not have a safer guide than the talented author of this work, who, by a residence of half a century, has practically grasped the habits, manners, and social conditions of the colonists he describes. All who wish to form a fair idea of the difficulties and pleasures of life in a new country, unlike England in some respects, yet like it in many, should read this book."—*John Bull.*

XIII.—DARIEN; OR, THE MERCHANT PRINCE.

BY ELIOT WARBURTON.

"This last production of the author of 'The Crescent and the Cross' has the same elements of a very wide popularity. It will please its thousands."—*Globe.*

"Eliot Warburton's active and productive genius is amply exemplified in the present book. We have seldom met with any work in which the realities of history and the poetry of fiction were more happily interwoven "—*Illustrated News.*

XIV.—FAMILY ROMANCE; OR, DOMESTIC ANNALS OF THE ARISTOCRACY.

BY SIR BERNARD BURKE, ULSTER KING OF ARMS.

"It were impossible to praise too highly this most interesting book, whether we should have regard to its excellent plan or its not less excellent execution. It ought to be found on every drawing-room table. Here you have nearly fifty captivating romances with the pith of all their interest preserved in undiminished poignancy, and any one may be read in half an hour. It is not the least of their merits that the romances are founded on fact —or what, at least, has been handed down for truth by long tradition—and the romance of reality far exceeds the romance of fiction."—*Standard.*

XV.—THE LAIRD OF NORLAW.

BY MRS. OLIPHANT.

"We have had frequent opportunities of commending Messrs. Hurst and Blackett's Standard Library. For neatness, elegance, and distinctness the volumes in this series surpass anything with which we are familiar. 'The Laird of Norlaw' will fully sustain the author's high reputation. The reader is carried on from first to last with an energy of sympathy that never flags."—*Sunday Times.*

"'The Laird of Norlaw' is worthy of the author's reputation. It is one of the most exquisite of modern novels."—*Observer.*

XVI.—THE ENGLISHWOMAN IN ITALY.

BY MRS. G. GRETTON.

"Mrs. Gretton had opportunities which rarely fall to the lot of strangers of becoming acquainted with the inner life and habits of a part of the Italian peninsula which is the very centre of the national crisis. We can praise her performance as interesting, unexaggerated, and full of opportune instruction."—*The Times.*

"Mrs. Gretton's book is timely, life-like, and for every reason to be recommended. It is impossible to close the book without liking the writer as well as the subject. The work is engaging, because real."—*Athenæum.*

11

XVII.—NOTHING NEW.

BY THE AUTHOR OF "JOHN HALIFAX, GENTLEMAN."

"'Nothing New' displays all those superior merits which have made 'John Halifax' one of the most popular works of the day. There is a force and truthfulness about these tales which mark them as the production of no ordinary mind, and we cordially recommend them to the perusal of all lovers of fiction."—*Morning Post.*

XVIII.—LIFE OF JEANNE D'ALBRET, QUEEN OF NAVARRE.

BY MISS FREER.

"We have read this book with great pleasure, and have no hesitation in recommending it to general perusal. It reflects the highest credit on the industry and ability of Miss Freer. Nothing can be more interesting than her story of the life of Jeanne D'Albret and the narrative is as trustworthy as it is attractive."—*Morning Post.*

XIX.—THE VALLEY OF A HUNDRED FIRES.

BY THE AUTHOR OF "MARGARET AND HER BRIDESMAIDS."

"If asked to classify this work, we should give it a place between 'John Halifax' and 'The Caxtons.'"—*Standard.*
"The spirit in which the whole book is written is refined and good."—*Athenæum.*
"This is in every sense a charming novel."—*Messenger.*

XX.—THE ROMANCE OF THE FORUM; OR, NARRATIVES, SCENES, AND ANECDOTES FROM COURTS OF JUSTICE.

BY PETER BURKE, SERJEANT AT LAW.

"This attractive book will be perused with much interest. It contains a great variety of singular and highly romantic stories."—*John Bull.*
"A work of singular interest, which can never fail to charm and absorb the reader's attention. The present cheap and elegant edition includes the true story of the Colleen Bawn."—*Illustrated News.*

XXI.—ADÈLE.

BY JULIA KAVANAGH.

"'Adèle' is the best work we have read by Miss Kavanagh; it is a charming story, full of delicate character-painting. The interest kindled in the first chapter burns brightly to the close."—*Athenæum.*
"'Adèle' will fully sustain the reputation of Miss Kavanagh, high as it already ranks."—*John Bull.*
"'Adèle' is a love-story of very considerable pathos and power. It a a very clever novel."—*Daily News.*

XXII.—STUDIES FROM LIFE.

BY THE AUTHOR OF "JOHN HALIFAX, GENTLEMAN."

"These 'Studies' are truthful and vivid pictures of life, often earnest, always full o. right feeling, and occasionally lightened by touches of quiet, genial humour. The volume is remarkable for thought, sound sense, shrewd observation, and kind and sympathetic feeling for all things good and beautiful."—*Morning Post.*
"These 'Studies from Life' are remarkable for graphic power and observation. The book will not diminish the reputation of the accomplished author."—*Saturday Review.*

HURST & BLACKETT'S STANDARD LIBRARY

XXIII.—GRANDMOTHER'S MONEY.

BY F. W. ROBINSON.

"We commend 'Grandmother's Money' to readers in search of a good novel. The characters are true to human nature, and the story is interesting."—*Athenæum.*

XXIV.—A BOOK ABOUT DOCTORS.

BY JOHN CORDY JEAFFRESON.

"A book to be read and re-read; fit for the study as well as the drawing-room table and the circulating library."—*Lancet.*
"This is a pleasant book for the fireside season, and for the seaside season. Mr. Jeaffreson has, out of hundreds of volumes, collected thousands of good things, adding thereto much that appears in print for the first time, and which, of course, gives increased value to this very readable book."—*Athenæum.*

XXV.—NO CHURCH.

BY F. W. ROBINSON.

"We advise all who have the opportunity to read this book. It is well worth the study."—*Athenæum.*
"A work of great originality, merit, and power."—*Standard.*

XXVI.—MISTRESS AND MAID.

BY THE AUTHOR OF "JOHN HALIFAX, GENTLEMAN."

"A good wholesome book, gracefully written, and as pleasant to read as it is instructive."—*Athenæum.*
"A charming tale, charmingly told."—*Standard.*
"All lovers of a good novel will hail with delight another of Mrs. Craik's charming stories."—*John Bull.*

XXVII.—LOST AND SAVED.

BY THE HON. MRS. NORTON.

"'Lost and Saved' will be read with eager interest by those who love a touching story It is a vigorous novel."—*Times.*
"This story is animated, full of exciting situations and stirring incidents. The characters are delineated with great power. Above and beyond these elements of a good novel, here is that indefinable charm with which true genius invests all it touches."—*Daily News.*

XXVIII.—LES MISERABLES.

BY VICTOR HUGO.

Authorised Copyright English Translation.

"The merits of 'Les Miserables' do not merely consist in the conception of it as a whole; it abounds with details of unequalled beauty. M. Victor Hugo has stamped upon every page the hall-mark of genius."—*Quarterly Review.*

XXIX.—BARBARA'S HISTORY

BY AMELIA B. EDWARDS.

"It is not often that we light upon a novel of so much merit and interes as 'Barbara's History.' It is a work conspicuous for taste and literary culture. It is a very graceful and charming book, with a well-managed story, clearly-cut characters, and sentiments expressed with an exquisite elocution. The dialogues especially sparkle with repartee. It is a book which the world will like. This is high praise of a work of art, and so we intend it."—*The Times.*

13

XXX.—LIFE OF THE REV. EDWARD IRVING.

BY MRS. OLIPHANT.

"A good book on a most interesting theme."—*Times.*
"A truly interesting and most affecting memoir. 'Irving's Life' ought to have a niche in every gallery of religious biography. There are few lives that will be fuller of instruction, interest, and consolation."—*Saturday Review.*

XXXI.—ST. OLAVE'S.

BY THE AUTHOR OF " JANITA'S CROSS."

"This novel is the work of one who possesses a great talent for writing, as well as experience and knowledge of the world. The whole book is worth reading."—*Athenæum.*
"'St. Olave's' belongs to a lofty order of fiction. It is a good novel, but it is something more. It is written with unflagging ability, and it is as even as it is clever. The author has determined to do nothing short of the best, and has succeeded."—*Morning Post.*

XXXII.—SAM SLICK'S TRAITS OF AMERICAN HUMOUR.

"Dip where you will into this lottery of fun, you are sure to draw out a prize. These Traits ' exhibit most successfully the broad national features of American humour."—*Post.*

XXXIII.—CHRISTIAN'S MISTAKE.

BY THE AUTHOR OF " JOHN HALIFAX, GENTLEMAN."

"A more charming story has rarely been written. It is a choice gift to be able thus to render human nature so truly, to penetrate its depths with such a searching sagacity, and to illuminate them with a radiance so eminently the writer's own."—*Times.*

XXXIV.—ALEC FORBES OF HOWGLEN.

BY GEORGE MAC DONALD, LL.D.

"No account of this story would give any idea of the profound interest that pervades the work from the first page to the last."—*Athenæum.*
"A novel of uncommon merit. Sir Walter Scott said he would advise no man to try to read 'Clarissa Harlowe' out loud in company if he wished to keep his character for manly superiority to tears. We fancy a good many hardened old novel-readers will feel a rising in the throat as they follow the fortunes of Alec and Annie."—*Pall Mall Gazette.*

XXXV.—AGNES.

BY MRS. OLIPHANT.

"'Agnes" is a novel superior to any of Mrs. Oliphant's former works."—*Athenæum.*
"Mrs. Oliphant is one of the most admirable of our novelists. In her works there are always to be found high principle, good taste, sense, and refinement. 'Agnes' is a story whose pathetic beauty will appeal irresistibly to all readers."—*Morning Post.*

XXXVI.—A NOBLE LIFE.

BY THE AUTHOR OF " JOHN HALIFAX, GENTLEMAN."

"Few men and no women will read 'A Noble Life' without feeling themselves the better for the effort."—*Spectator.*
"A beautifully written and touching tale. It is a noble book."—*Morning Post.*
"'A Noble Life' is remarkable for the high types of character it presents, and the skill with which they are made to work out a story of powerful and pathetic interest."
—*Daily News.*

XXXVII—NEW AMERICA.

BY W. HEPWORTH DIXON.

"A very interesting book. Mr. Dixon has written thoughtfully and well."—*Times.*
"We recommend everyone who feels any interest in human nature to read Mr. Dixon's very interesting book."—*Saturday Review.*

HURST & BLACKETT'S STANDARD LIBRARY

XXXVIII.—ROBERT FALCONER.

BY GEORGE MAC DONALD, LL.D.

"'Robert Falconer' is a work brimful of life and humour and of the deepest human interest. It is a book to be returned to again and again for the deep and searching knowledge it evinces of human thoughts and feelings."—*Athenæum.*

XXXIX.—THE WOMAN'S KINGDOM.

BY THE AUTHOR OF "JOHN HALIFAX, GENTLEMAN."

"'The Woman's Kingdom' sustains the author's reputation as a writer of the purest and noblest kind of domestic stories."—*Athenæum.*
"'The Woman's Kingdom' is remarkable for its romantic interest. The characters are masterpieces. Edna is worthy of the hand that drew John Halifax."—*Morning Post.*

XL.—ANNALS OF AN EVENTFUL LIFE.

BY GEORGE WEBBE DASENT, D.C.L.

"A racy, well-written, and original novel. The interest never flags. The whole work sparkles with wit and humour."—*Quarterly Review.*

XLI—DAVID ELGINBROD.

BY GEORGE MAC DONALD, LL.D.

"A novel which is the work of a man of genius. It will attract the highest class of readers."—*Times.*

XLII.—A BRAVE LADY.

BY THE AUTHOR OF "JOHN HALIFAX, GENTLEMAN."

"We earnestly recommend this novel. It is a special and worthy specimen of the author's remarkable powers. The reader's attention never for a moment flags."—*Post.*
"'A Brave Lady' thoroughly rivets the unmingled sympathy of the reader, and her history deserves to stand foremost among the author's works."—*Daily Telegraph.*

XLIII.—HANNAH.

BY THE AUTHOR OF "JOHN HALIFAX, GENTLEMAN."

"A very pleasant, healthy story, well and artistically told. The book is sure of a wide circle of readers. The character of Hannah is one of rare beauty."—*Standard.*
"A powerful novel of social and domestic life. One of the most successful efforts of a successful novelist."—*Daily News.*

XLIV.—SAM SLICK'S AMERICANS AT HOME.

"This is one of the most amusing books that we ever read."—*Standard.*
"'The Americans at Home' will not be less popular than any of Judge Halliburton's previous works."—*Morning Post.*

XLV.—THE UNKIND WORD.

BY THE AUTHOR OF "JOHN HALIFAX, GENTLEMAN."

"These stories are gems of narrative. Indeed, some of them, in their touching grace and simplicity, seem to us to possess a charm even beyond the authoress's most popular novels. Of none of them can this be said more emphatically than of that which opens the series. 'The Unkind Word.' It is wonderful to see the imaginative power displayed in the few delicate touches by which this successful love-story is sketched out."—*The Echo.*

HURST & BLACKETT'S STANDARD LIBRARY

XLVI.—A ROSE IN JUNE.

BY MRS. OLIPHANT.

"'A Rose in June' is as pretty as its title. The story is one of the best and most touching which we owe to the industry and talent of Mrs. Oliphant, and may hold its own with even 'The Chronicles of Carlingford.'"—*Times.*

XLVII.—MY LITTLE LADY.

BY E. FRANCES POYNTER.

"This story presents a number of vivid and very charming pictures Indeed, the whole book is charming. It is interesting in both character and story, and thoroughly good of its kind."—*Saturday Review.*

XLVIII.—PHŒBE, JUNIOR.

BY MRS. OLIPHANT.

"This last 'Chronicle of Carlingford' not merely takes rank fairly beside the first which introduced us to 'Salem Chapel,' but surpasses all the intermediate records. Phœbe, Junior, herself is admirably drawn."—*Academy.*

XLIX.—LIFE OF MARIE ANTOINETTE.

BY PROFESSOR CHARLES DUKE YONGE.

"A work of remarkable merit and interest, which will, we doubt not, become the most popular English history of Marie Antoinette."—*Spectator.*

L.—SIR GIBBIE.

BY GEORGE MAC DONALD, LL.D.

"'Sir Gibbie' is a book of genius."—*Pall Mall Gazette.*
"This book has power, pathos, and humour."—*Athenæum.*

LI.—YOUNG MRS. JARDINE.

BY THE AUTHOR OF "JOHN HALIFAX, GENTLEMAN."

"'Young Mrs. Jardine' is a pretty story, written in pure English."—*The Times.*
"There is much good feeling in this book. It is pleasant and wholesome."—*Athenæum.*

LII.—LORD BRACKENBURY.

BY AMELIA B. EDWARDS.

"A very readable story. The author has well conceived the purpose of high-class novel-writing, and succeeded in no small measure in attaining it. There is plenty of variety, cheerful dialogue, and general 'verve' in the book."—*Athenæum.*

LIII.—IT WAS A LOVER AND HIS LASS.

BY MRS. OLIPHANT.

"In 'It was a Lover and his Lass,' we admire Mrs. Oliphant exceedingly. It would be worth reading a second time, were it only for the sake of one ancient Scottish spinster, who is nearly the counterpart of the admirable Mrs. Margaret Maitland."—*Times.*

LIV.—THE REAL LORD BYRON—THE STORY OF THE POET'S LIFE.

BY JOHN CORDY JEAFFRESON.

"Mr. Jeaffreson comes forward with a narrative which must take a very important place in Byronic literature; and it may reasonably be anticipated that this book will be regarded with deep interest by all who are concerned in the works and the fame of this great English poet."—*The Times.*

16

www.ingramcontent.com/pod-product-compliance
Lightning Source LLC
Chambersburg PA
CBHW020943030726
47496CB00005B/1331